Renew by pho
0845 0020

D0262061

Always a Hero

Always a Hero

JUSTINE DAVIS

First published in Great Britain 2011
by Mills & Boon, an imprint of Harlequin (UK) Limited.
Large Print edition 2011
Harlequin (UK) Limited,
Eton House, 18-24 Paradise Road,
Richmond, Surrey TW9 1SR

© Janice Davis Smith 2011

ISBN: 978 0 263 22349 1

Harlequin (UK) policy is to use papers that are natural,
renewable and recyclable products and made from
wood grown in sustainable forests. The logging
and manufacturing process conform to the legal
environmental regulations of the country of origin.

Printed and bound in Great Britain
by CPI Antony Rowe, Chippenham, Wiltshire

JUSTINE DAVIS

lives on Puget Sound in Washington. Her interests outside of writing are sailing, doing needlework, horseback riding and driving her restored 1967 Corvette roadster—top down, of course.

Justine says that years ago, during her career in law enforcement, a young man she worked with encouraged her to try for a promotion to a position that was at the time occupied only by men. "I succeeded, became wrapped up in my new job, and that man moved away, never, I thought, to be heard from again. Ten years later he appeared out of the woods of Washington state, saying he'd never forgotten me and would I please marry him. With that history, how could I write anything but romance?"

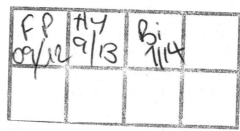

To all of those who,
in whatever kind of uniform,
stand between us and the dark side.

Chapter 1

"I hate you! I hate this place. I want to go home."

"I know. Just do it."

Jordan Price threw down the rake, scattering the leaves he'd just gathered. His father chose not to point out that he'd just guaranteed himself more time spent in the task he loathed.

"I'm never going to be such a jerk to my kids."

Wyatt Blake smothered a sigh, but managed to keep his tone reasonable; he remembered thinking much worse thoughts about his own father. And at younger than thirteen, too.

So that's how you want you and Jordan to be? Like you and your father?

He fought down his gut reaction and spoke calmly.

"If you don't learn to finish what you start, your kids won't listen to you anyway. If you can even find a woman who'd have them with a man who doesn't keep his word."

Yeah, right. You're such an expert on keeping promises.

"I don't know why Mom married you anyway."

"It's a mystery. Finish."

The grumbling continued, with a couple of words muttered under the boy's breath that Wyatt decided not to hear. He had enough on his plate at the moment, trying to keep the kid out of serious trouble, without expending energy on his language. If he didn't straighten around soon, a few obscenities would be the least of his problems.

Later, when after another battle Jordan had gone to bed, Wyatt went through his nightly ritual at the computer that sat in the corner of the den. Jordan wasn't allowed to have it in his room, another bone of contention. But tonight something disrupted the usual process; a message alert window popped up. One he had hoped he'd never see.

He went still. Maybe it was a mistake, a computer glitch. They were prone to that, one-time, inexplicable weirdness.

For a long moment he did nothing, postponing the inevitable. A measure of how far he'd come, he supposed, that he didn't dive in instantly.

Finally, knowing he had no choice, he began the digging process that would take him to the program buried deep within the computer's file structure. There was no convenient icon for this one, no listing on the menus, no easy way to get there. And once he was there, the encryption was so deep it would take him five minutes to work his way through all the levels.

Assuming he could remember the damned process, let alone the multiple passwords.

In the end it took him six minutes and change. But at last the screen opened. The message was short. Far too short to have the effect it did.

Old acquaintance asking for you. Afraid I gave him wrong directions, but maybe he'll

*find you anyway. Was a friendly when you
knew him, but keep your eyes open.*

He stared at the unsigned message. He didn't
need a signature, there was only one person
who knew how to contact him this way. Who
knew how to contact him at all. When he'd left
that world he'd literally cashed out, cutting all
ties. The man who'd sent him this email had
spent a great deal of time convincing him to
agree to this one thin thread of connection.

The message was innocuous enough on the
surface, but he knew better. It was a warning
as surely as if it were a fire alarm.

He'd spent most of his adult life knowing his
past could catch up with him someday. That
past held too many grim memories for him to
relish the idea, but that didn't change the possibility. He'd always looked upon it as a cost of
doing business, his business at least.

But now there was Jordan, and that changed
everything.

Knowing there was nothing more to be
gained by staring at this unexpected jab from
the past, he quickly typed one word that would
serve as both acknowledgment and thanks, and

sent it. Then he deleted the message, reset the encryption and exited. The small but sophisticated program would erase its own tracks as it went, and go back into hiding.

He had a little time, thanks to the misdirection, but he'd have to redouble his watchfulness. In the meantime, with that ability to compartmentalize that had worked so well for him back in those days, he returned to his original task.

When the social networking site was loaded, Wyatt called up the usual page and without a qualm entered the password Jordan didn't know he knew. Then he hit the next link in the process.

My father has to be the most boring guy on the planet.

The first post since he'd last checked glowed at him.

Wyatt didn't wince, even inwardly, at the damning—at least in a thirteen-year-old's view—indictment. In fact, he felt a certain satisfaction. Boredom, he'd often thought, was highly underrated.

He went on reading, scrolling through the entries from where he'd left off last week. Jordan, of course, had no idea he knew the page existed. The boy had never asked if he could do it, had just set it up on his own shortly after they'd moved in. Perhaps he'd known if he'd asked the answer would be no. Better to beg forgiveness later and all that.

And that thought did make him wince. Hadn't he lived by that credo himself, often enough?

And now Wyatt was glad he'd done it, and was using it against him. At least, that's what Jordan would think. He went back to reading. He noticed the new friends added, made a note of a meet-up Jordan had been invited to next Saturday night. Invited several times by several people Wyatt already had been wary of after checking their respective pages. He didn't like the sound of it, so he'd have to make sure his son was otherwise occupied.

He kept reading, and reached the final post.

I hate him. I wish he was dead and my mom was still alive.

The last entry sat there, unchanging, undeniable. He blinked. Closed the browser. Shut down the computer. Got up from the desk.

Walked up the stairs. Opened the first door on the right.

Jordan lay curled up on his side, like his mother had said he used to sleep when he'd been much, much smaller. The room was a mess, clothes strewn about, belongings scattered. But he was there, and for the moment, safe. Wyatt went on down the hall to his own room.

Mechanically he went through the rituals of getting ready for sleep, as if that would help it come, or that it would be restful when it did. He knew what would happen. He would lie down, resisting the urge to draw up in a fetal curl himself. And then it would begin, the nightly parade of images and memories. And if he was really exhausted, the idea would occur to him that all the people around the world who had damned him were getting their wish.

He turned out the bedside light. His head hit the pillow.

He closed his eyes, wondering if this would be one of the nights he regretted going to sleep. In the silence of the house, broken only by the occasional creak or snap as it contracted in the rapidly chilling night air, the latest in the long string of confrontations played back in his head. He thought of all the things he'd done, all the places he'd been, all the situations he'd faced, all the times when he'd been written off as dead or likely to be.

He'd survived them all.

But he wasn't at all sure he was going to survive a thirteen-year-old boy.

I hate him. I wish he was dead and my mom was still alive.

"So do I," he whispered into the darkness.

Kai Reynolds heard the guitar riff signal from the front door of Play On as she got to the last line of the vendor form. She'd rigged the system to rotate through a series of recorded bits daily. This week it was the classics. Yesterday had been a few seconds of Stevie Ray, today was The Edge on her fave, that sweet Fender Strat, tomorrow would be the simplest and oldest, that classic single chord from George Harrison's Rickenbacker 12-string that opened "A Hard Day's Night."

Next week it would be some Wylde, Rivers

Cuomo and Mustaine balanced by a variety pack of Atkins and Robert Johnson leavened with a bit of Urban.

She took three seconds to finish checking the order against her inventory of guitar strings, then looked up. She quickly spotted who had come in, one who didn't often have to ask because he usually knew, even from the three- to five-second clips, who was playing. For a kid his age, Jordan Price had a good ear.

An idea struck her, that she should add in some people he might not know. Ry Cooder, maybe, or Derek Trucks. And to bolster the feminine side, some of Raitt's sweet slide and Batten's two-handed tapping.

"Hey, Kai," Jordan said, his face lighting up when he saw her behind the counter.

"Jordy," she acknowledged with a return smile. The boy had told her some time ago, rather shyly, that he allowed no one else to use that nickname. She knew he had a bit of a crush on her, so she'd gently told him that someday he'd meet another girl he didn't mind it from, and then he'd know she was the one.

"The Edge, right? The Stratocaster?"

"Right in one," she said, her smile becoming a grin.

"You oughta put you in there."

Her smile became a grin at the words he said at least two or three days a week when he came in after school. "Nah. I'm not in their league."

"But that riff you did on *Crash,* that was killer."

"I borrowed it from Knopfler."

"But yours sounded completely different."

"That was the Gibson, not me," she said, as if they hadn't had this conversation before. "What did you do, run all the way?"

The boy walked from the middle school that was about a mile away. Then, when he was done, he walked back to school, usually in haste, before his father got there to pick him up. She thought it odd, since she was closer to where the boy lived than the school was, but Jordy said his father insisted because he didn't trust him.

"Should he?" she'd asked.

"Sure," Jordy had answered, his expression grim. "Where am I gonna go in this town?"

There had been a wealth of disdain in his voice, but Kai had let it pass.

"Nah, it's just hot out today," he said now.

"Enjoy it. Fall's hovering." The boy made a face. "Maybe we'll get snow this winter."

His expression changed slightly, looking the tiniest bit intrigued, as she'd guessed a kid who'd grown up in Southern California might at the idea.

"That would be cool," he said, then smiled at his own unintentional pun.

"So how's life today?"

"Sucks," Jordy said, his smile fading.

"Still not getting along with your dad, huh?"

"He's an as—" Jordy broke off what had obviously been going to be a crude bodily assessment.

"Good save," Kai said, acknowledging the effort. "Your mom probably didn't like you swearing."

"Only reason I stopped," Jordy muttered, looking away. Kai guessed he was tearing up and didn't want her to see.

"If we can't cry for the ones we've loved and lost, then what good are we?" she asked softly.

He looked up at her then, and she indeed saw
the gleam of moisture in his eyes. Those green
eyes, she thought, were going to knock that girl
he'd meet someday right on her backside.

"You understand, because you lost someone,
too."

The boy not only had a good ear, he was perceptive.

"Yes."

"Kit."

She didn't talk about him, ever. But this was
a kid in pain, worse today than she'd ever seen
it, and she sensed he needed to know he wasn't
alone. And she suspected he already knew how
Christopher Hudson had died; the info was out
there, on the Net, and easy enough to find.

"Yes. And I loved him very much," she finally said. "But it wasn't like your mother, who
didn't want to leave you. He did it to himself."

Jordy's eyes widened. "He killed himself?"

No outside source would have said that, she
knew. They all said it was accidental. She
didn't look at it that way. But then, she'd been
in the middle of it.

"Slowly. Years of drugs."

"Oh." Jordy was silent for a moment before he said, in a small voice, "How long ago?"

She hesitated again. Was he wondering how long it took to feel life was worth living again?

"A long time ago." Six years ago was almost half his lifetime, so she figured that was accurate. "And," she added quietly, "yesterday."

She saw his brows furrow, then clear as he nodded slowly in understanding.

"So you haven't…forgotten?"

Panic edged his voice. Ah, she thought. So that was it. "No. And I never will. And you won't either, Jordy. I promise you."

"But…sometimes I can't remember what she sounded like."

Interesting, she thought, that it was sound and not image that he was worried about.

"But do you remember how you felt when she talked to you, told you how much she loved you?"

The boy colored slightly, but nodded again.

"Then you remember the important part. And you always will."

It was a few minutes before the boy got around to asking if he could have the sound room and the slightly battered but well-loved Strat she often let people use. Jordan was just starting out, and it was a bit too much for his hands. She had a small acoustic in back she thought he'd do better with, but he thought acoustics were boring and wasn't interested. Yet.

Now there was something to add to the door rotation, she thought. Some of her personal favorite acoustic bits, six- and twelve-string, Steve Davison and Jaquie Gipson first on the list, Kaki too, and John Butler and his custom eleven strings. Nobody could listen to them and still think acoustics were boring.

But in the meantime, the boy wanted the solace that laboriously plinking out chords until his fingers were sore brought him.

"No," she said to his request, startling him; she'd never declined him before. But at her gesture he followed her into the former storage room she'd had converted into a soundproof room with a small recording system set up. Nothing fancy, but enough for accurate and fairly full playback. The conversion had cost her, but it had paid for itself by the third year; not many aspiring players could resist the temptation of purchasing the instrument they liked best once they'd heard the sound played back for them. There was something about the process that was an incredible selling tool.

Jordy followed her into the room, knowing to dodge the corner of the keyboard in the slightly cramped space before she even flipped the lights on. She walked across to the rack where she'd put the Gibson SG when she'd finished last night; the mood had been upon her and she'd indulged in a rare these days midnight jam, playing riff after riff until her own out-of-practice fingers were sore.

She picked up the gleaming blue guitar and held it out to the boy.

"Try this one."

The boy's eyes widened and she heard him smother a gulping breath. "BeeGee?"

She grinned at his use of her old nickname for the guitar, B for the color, and G for Gibson. A name she'd come up with before it had been pointed out to her that she'd inadvertently chosen the name of her mother's favorite group, back in the day. It had taken her a while to get over the humiliation of that, but the name had stuck.

And the gesture had the result she'd wanted; the boy completely forgot the pain he'd been mired in. For the moment, he would be all right.

She closed the door behind her, thinking it might be better if she couldn't hear what sounds his untrained fingers might coax out of her baby. The neck was small enough, but it tended to be a bit head-heavy and might give him trouble. Maybe it would teach him that form had a big role in function; right now he was too taken with looks and flash to absorb that.

When she got back into the store she found Mrs. Ogilvie waiting, a new book of piano music in her hands. Marilyn was desperate to get her youngest daughter seriously interested, although Kai knew Jessica couldn't care less. At sixteen, her life was full of other things. But her mother kept trying, and Kai wondered if at some point, despite the steady stream of money, she should try and explain that some people just didn't have the desire or the talent.

Maybe I should suggest she take lessons herself, Kai thought. *Then at least somebody would get some use out of all these books.*

"I saw Wyatt's boy come in," Marilyn said as she rang up the sale.

"He comes in almost every day," Kai said. Marilyn glanced around questioningly. "He's in the sound room," Kai explained. "Practicing."

Marilyn sniffed audibly. "At least he *will* practice. Is he taking lessons?"

"He'd like to, but his father won't let him. I guess he's pretty strict."

"Now that's hard to believe," Marilyn said with a laugh.

Marilyn would have likely known Jordy's dad, Kai realized; she'd lived here for most of her life. She, having only been here four years, knew nothing about him outside of Jordy's litany of complaints.

All he does is work and hassle me, the boy had told her once. She remembered smiling at the typical complaint, one she'd made about her own father before she'd grown up enough to appreciate the love behind both actions.

"You remember him?" Kai asked, curious to see if there was another viewpoint on the man, curious enough to endure Marilyn's rather scattered conversational style. "From before, I mean?"

"Wyatt Blake? Anybody who lived in Deer Creek then remembers Wyatt. Smart, restless, and reckless. When he left town at seventeen, nobody was surprised. We all felt bad for Tim and Claire though. Tim was strict, but Wyatt needed that, reckless as he was."

This hardly fit with Jordy's description, Kai thought. But people changed. Or maybe that was why he was strict with Jordy, because it was all he knew.

"They were good to that boy," Marilyn added, "worked hard to give him a good life, and he still couldn't wait to get out of here. They almost never heard from him. Then when it's too late for them, he shows up back here, a widower with a young son, and won't even talk about it. Why, I tried to tell him how sorry I was, and he wouldn't have any of it."

"Maybe he didn't want any pity or sympathy."

"But he was downright rude about it. Claire would never have stood for that."

"Seems like he learned from them after all, though," Kai said. "Jordy says he works hard."

And boring work, Jordy had added, as if it were a crime.

"Yes," Marilyn said.

"And he did come back home."

Marilyn brightened at that. "Yes. Yes, he did. Not a word out of him about where he's been or what he's been doing for more than twenty years, but he did come home. Moved himself and the boy back into their old house."

As the woman later went on her way, Kai wondered yet again why people had kids at all. Seemed to just be asking for pain and tears.

I should call Mom, she thought. *Let her tell me again how it was all worth it.*

Except that that would be followed by the inevitable lecture, very wearing considering she'd been so consumed by Play On that she'd barely had time to breathe, let alone date. But it didn't stop her mom from declaring it was time she found a good man and settled down to the task of a family herself. The very idea still gave her the shivers. She liked kids well enough, but babies made her very, very nervous. And she couldn't imagine sending a baby to sleep with a smoking riff on BeeGee; they needed soft, lullaby stuff. Someday, maybe. But that day was a long way off.

Not to mention there was that "good man" problem.

The Edge modulated his way through that six-note arpeggio again as the door opened. A man stepped in, a stranger to her, and she almost grinned at the juxtaposition of his sudden appearance and her own thoughts. Especially since he certainly had the looking part of good down. His hair was a little short for her taste, but she liked the sandy blond color. And he had that body type she liked—lean, wiry. And just tall enough; she liked a man she had to look up at even in heels, but not get a neck ache doing it.

He glanced around the store, quickly, almost assessingly, in a way that was somehow disconcerting. She had the odd thought that if she made him close his eyes and describe it to her, he'd get it perfectly, down to the Deer

Creek High School Musical poster on the wall behind him.

And he moves like a big cat, she thought as the man began to walk toward the back of the store. All grace and coiled power.

She shook her head, laughing inwardly at herself.

It's because he's a stranger, she told herself. Deer Creek was a small enough town that she'd seen most of the men around, and none had even come close to sparking such a sudden interest.

He paused for a moment to look at the one personal souvenir she'd allowed herself here; a photograph of her onstage at the peak of Relative Fusion's brief but promising existence, playing a packed, full-size arena for the first time. For her it had been the pinnacle, a height she would never see again, because Kit had tumbled off the high wire he'd been walking soon after that night, and her charmed life as she'd known it had ended.

She slid off the stool she'd been sitting on and took a couple of steps toward the man. She put on her best helpful smile, and in a tone to match she asked, "Help you find something?"

"Someone," the man said, still looking at the photograph.

Ooh, great voice, too, Kai thought. She had such a weakness for that rough, gravelly timbre.

Then he looked at her. Gave the photo another split-second glance.

"Never mind," he said, obviously realizing it was her in the photo, despite the fact that she had looked radically different in those days, with her hair long and wild and a ton of makeup and glitter on.

She met his gaze as this time he focused his attention on her unwaveringly. "You're Kai Reynolds."

Three things hit her in rapid-fire succession.

She was being assessed, in much the same way as his surroundings had been when he'd first come in.

Second, she knew those eyes. Jordy's eyes. The same vivid green, although somehow muted. Tired, she thought.

And at last came the realization. Impossibly, this was the stuffy, boring, staid Wyatt Blake.

And he was looking at her as if she'd crawled out from under the nearest rock.

Chapter 2

It was worse than he'd feared.

Wyatt stared at the young woman before him. He'd hoped, when he'd first seen the tidy, well-organized store that perhaps he'd been wrong to expect a problem here.

Play On hadn't been here when he'd lived here as a kid. He'd heard that the woman who owned and ran it had once been in a semi-successful rock band, which had registered only as an oddity in a little town like Deer Creek. But Mrs. Ogilvie—who had been the local information center when he was a teenager seemingly in trouble at every turn, and apparently still fulfilled that obligation—told him that Jordan came here after school almost every day, he'd known he had to check it out. Especially since Jordan had told him he was studying at school. He didn't like being lied to, especially by his own son. If this was going to work at all—and he had serious doubts about that—there had to be honesty between them.

The hypocrisy of that high-flown thought, given his own secrets, made him grimace.

"You're the owner," he said.

It came out more like an accusation than a question. He hadn't meant to sound so harsh, but his thoughts had put an edge in his voice.

She said nothing, but he'd spent his life gauging people's reactions, and as clearly as if she'd shouted it he knew he'd gotten her hackles up already. That wasn't how he'd wanted to approach this, but damn, she looked like his worst nightmare as far as Jordan was concerned. The rock-and-roll history was bad enough, but the slightly spiky red hair that fell forward to surround a face that managed to look sexy and impish at the same time, and the slim, intricate, knotted bracelet of a tattoo in a deep bluish-green color around her left wrist finished it for him. She would be an impossible-to-resist lure for an impressionable boy.

"Well?" he said, his voice even sharper.

"Was there a question?" she asked, her tone as cool as the steady gaze of smoky gray eyes. Whatever else she was, she wasn't easily intimidated.

He took a deep breath, and tried to rein it in. After all, she wasn't some rock gypsy any longer, was she? She'd quit that life, so maybe there was some sense behind those eyes.

The question was, how much of that life had she brought with her here?

"Where's the paraphernalia? In back?"

She blinked then, looking genuinely puzzled. "What?"

"The cigarette papers, the bongs, the glass pipes."

She went very still. The smoky gray eyes narrowed as she looked at him. "This is a music store, not a head shop."

"Right. And you never touched the stuff when you were a rock star."

She looked at him levelly. She was tall, he thought, five-eight or so. She wore black jeans and a gray shirt that had some sort of shine to it. Unremarkable, except for the way the shift and sheen of it subtly emphasized curves beneath it.

A subtle rocker? Hard to believe, he thought.

"As a matter of fact," she said icily, "I never did. And also as a matter of fact, I was never a rock star. I played in a band."

"A successful one."

"For a while."

"And you use that."

"Marketing," she said. "I'd be a fool not to, if I want to stay in business in a tough world." The practical assessment surprised him. "You have a problem with that?"

She was challenging him now.

"Only when you use it to lure in kids."

She went very still. When she spoke, her voice held a new edge that made him wary. "Lure?"

"Sexy girl rocker," he said. "If you're a teen-age boy there's not many lures bigger."

For an instant she looked startled. But her voice was no less edgy, and the edge sharpened as her words came bursting out.

"That dream died thanks to the kind of thing you're accusing me of selling. I would no more have drug paraphernalia here than I'd cook up meth in my kitchen."

At the fierceness of her voice Wyatt drew back slightly. Perhaps he should have done some research before he'd come charging in here. He didn't care for the way she was looking at him. Which was odd, since he'd come in here not caring what she thought, only wanting to find out what drew his son here day after day.

"You know," she said, "when Jordy told me his father did nothing but work and hassle him, I thought he was being a typical teenager. That his situation just made normal parenting seem like hassling. Seems I was wrong. You really are a…hard-ass."

Wyatt had the feeling Jordan had used another word, and he noted the fact that even angry she had not repeated it. He assumed a woman who'd lived in the rock world had much worse in her vocabulary, so either she'd censored herself because she didn't use the language with a potential customer, or because she was protecting Jordan.

Belatedly—much too belatedly—he realized that she knew he wasn't a potential customer at all, that she knew who he was.

"How did you know?"

To her credit, she didn't play dumb. "Please. Like there's more than two sets of those eyes in Deer Creek."

He blinked. He'd of course known Jordan had the same color eyes. It was one of the reasons, along with childhood pictures of each of them that could be interchangeable, that he'd never doubted Jordan was his son. He just hadn't expected a total stranger to notice it within five minutes.

And he hadn't wanted to tick off the one person in town that Jordan seemed to voluntarily gravitate to within that first five minutes, either. He wasn't even sure what had set him off. There had been a time when he'd been smoother, when he'd assessed a person accurately and chosen the right approach to get what information he needed from them.

Apparently that time was long past.

"Is my son here?" he asked, not even bothering to comment on her recognition.

"He's in back."

His brows furrowed as he glanced at the hallway behind her. "Doing what?"

"Smoking dope."

His gaze snapped back to her face.

"Isn't that what you expected?"

There was no denying the sour tone, or the annoyance in her voice.

And there was no denying that, if she was telling the truth, he had it coming. He just couldn't seem to find the right path on anything connected to Jordan.

With an effort he was almost too weary to make, he pulled his scattered thoughts together and made himself focus on the reason he was here and the best way to get what he needed from this woman, not the woman herself. It was surprisingly difficult. She had a presence, and he had the brief, flitting thought that she must have been something onstage.

"Ms. Reynolds," he said, trying to sound reasonable, "I'm just looking for my son."

"What you're doing," she said, "is driving him away."

"He'd have to be a lot closer before I could drive him away," he said wryly.

Something flickered in her eyes, whether at his rueful words or his tone he didn't know. But it was a better reaction than that fierce anger, or that icy cool, and he'd take it.

"Look, I just found out how much time Jordan spends here. I wanted to check the place out."

"So you come in with an attitude and a lot of assumptions?"

She had him there. "Yes," he admitted simply.

That won him the briefest trace of a smile.

"I'm sorry," he said, not realizing he was going to say it until the words were out.

"About which?" she asked, clearly requiring more than just a simple, blanket apology.

He looked at her for a moment. She held his gaze steadily. Nerve, he thought. Or else he'd lost his knack for intimidation entirely in the last year. Since that had been his goal he should be happy, not standing here missing the skill.

"The attitude," he said finally. "And the assumptions…they should have stayed at the possibilities stage."

"Every music store is a haven for druggies and their gear? A bit old-school, aren't you? Why risk it when people can get whatever they need or want online, with no open display of wares to get hassled over?"

She had, he knew, a very valid point. Several of them. He really should have thought more before he'd barged in here on the offensive.

"I was just worried about Jordan." He let out a long breath, lowering his gaze and shaking his head. "I pretty much suck at this father thing," he muttered.

"It's a tough gig."

The sudden gentleness of her tone caught him off guard. "I know this has been…difficult for him."

"Ya think?" she said. "His mom dies, the father he never knew shows up out of nowhere and proceeds to drag him back to that nowhere with him…well, nowhere in his view, anyway."

He'd been right about that, it seemed, Wyatt thought. Jordan talked to her. A lot. Certainly more than to him.

"I know he hates it here," he said.

"I know. 'It's too cold, half the roads aren't even paved, and there's hardly any people,'" she said, clearly quoting something Jordan had told her.

"That's exactly what I like about it," Wyatt said.

"The cold, the roads, or the lack of population?"

"Selection C."

Her brows rose. "So it's not just me who sets you off, it's people in general?"

He wasn't quite sure there wasn't something about her in particular, but he didn't want to delve into that now.

"I've seen what people can do."

For a moment she just looked at him. Then, with an odd sort of gentleness, she said, "I have, too. They can build skyscrapers, write incredible poetry and stories, and impossibly beautiful music. They can be kind and generous and pull together when others need them. They can weep at pain and sadness, or at a beautiful sunset."

He stared at her. "And they can inflict pain, murder and mayhem on each other."

She didn't flinch. "Yes. That too. Fascinating, isn't it?"

"You wouldn't say that if you'd ever had to deal with the reality."

Her gaze narrowed, and he regretted the words. And not for the implied criticism. Hastily he looked for something to divert the question he could sense was about to come.

"What kind of name is Kai?"

It sounded rude, and abrupt, but it accomplished the goal. Instead of asking what he knew about mayhem, she instead said sweetly, too sweetly he thought, "Mine."

Now that she'd been diverted, he backed off. "I mean, where did it come from?"

"My parents."

She wasn't obtuse, he already knew that, so she was paying him back for his attitude, he supposed. He also figured he had it coming.

"And what," he said evenly, "was their inspiration?"

She studied him for a moment before saying, "It's Kauai without the *u a*."

He blinked. "What?"

"Island in Hawaii? Fourth-largest? The Garden Isle?"

She was talking to him, he realized, as if he were the obtuse one. And he somewhat belatedly realized he would do well not to underestimate this woman.

"Were you born there?" That seemed a reasonable question, he thought.

"No. The fun part happened there."

His mouth quirked. And she smiled, a bright, beautiful smile, and much more than the tiny alteration in his own expression deserved.

"Mom shortened it to the one syllable, to avoid me having to remember what order all the vowels came in when I was little, a thoughtfulness I still thank her for."

The quirk became a smile of his own, he couldn't seem to help it. And when he asked this time, the attitude was missing.

"What's Jordan really doing?"

"Playing."

He blinked. "Playing. Video games? Poker? Bingo?"

She didn't take offense this time. Instead, the

smile became a grin, and it hit him somewhere near the solar plexus and nearly took his breath away.

"A Gibson SG."

"A guitar?"

"That one, to be exact," she said, gesturing at the photograph he'd seen near the guitar display.

He didn't have to turn to look; the image seemed to have been seared into his mind. But he only vaguely remembered the blue guitar. What he remembered was the flash and lighting pouring down over the stage, creating a sort of halo around the woman—a girl, really—in a sleek, black outfit that looked painted over long legs, sweet curves, and a tossed mane of red hair. Brighter, longer, and wilder than her hair now, it gleamed like wildfire with the backlighting.

"He's playing a guitar," he repeated, to be sure he'd heard right. "Your guitar."

"Seemed like he'd had a bad day. Thought it might cheer him up."

"I didn't... He's really playing?"

"Well, he's trying. Practicing. Hard. He really wants to learn."

Since he hadn't seen Jordan try hard at a damn thing, Wyatt was more than a little taken aback. "Since when?"

She looked thoughtful for a moment. "I'd say he started coming in about six months ago."

About a month after he'd returned to Deer Creek, Jordan in tow.

"You didn't know he was interested?"

He shook his head. "His mother never said."

She looked at him consideringly, no doubt wondering why he hadn't known himself, without being told. But all she said was, "I'm sorry, it must have been awful, her dying like that."

"Yes." It had been awful. Painful and hard, and those last days when Melissa had been in such an anxious rush to tell him all he needed to know were days he would never forget.

"He misses her."

"I know."

"You don't," she said, eyeing him with that assessing look again.

"I barely knew her."

"Well enough to have a child with her."

He wasn't about to explain *that* complicated story to this woman he'd just met.

"My mistake," he said.

He saw the abruptness of his answer register. But when she spoke it wasn't in response to that.

"Do you know your son any better?"

"No," he admitted, his earlier frustration rising anew.

"Maybe if you'd ever had anything to do with him, you'd be in a better place with him now."

She didn't say it accusingly, but it bit deep just the same. He didn't make excuses, ever. He'd been determined not to discuss this with anyone, for Jordan's sake if nothing else, and he certainly didn't want to do it here and now and with this woman. But the pressure of not being able to handle one thirteen-year-old boy, he who had handled far worse, was wearing him down. And for the second time since he'd walked in here, words he'd never intended to say surged out.

"Hard to do when until seven months ago I never even knew he existed."

Chapter 3

Kai stared at the man standing on the other side of the counter. So many impressions were tumbling through her mind that she'd almost forgotten her first one, that those eyes, Jordy's vivid green eyes, looked far too exhausted for a man in his line of work.

Jordy's whine—because the long, wound-up complaint had indeed been that—echoed in her head. *He's a pill counter. He counts how many packages of cold pills they put in the boxes. How lame is that? And he wouldn't even have that job if old man Hunt didn't owe him a favor.*

She had understood Jordy's anger about his life, agreed he had a right to be upset, having been uprooted from the only home he knew and dragged a thousand miles away, away from his school, his friends. But this had hit a hot button with her, and it had been an effort to answer quietly.

"My dad worked in a canning plant once," she'd told him. "Dead fish all day. He hated it. But he did it. Because he had a family to take care of, because he wanted me to have a roof over my head and food on the table. It's called responsibility, Jordy. It's called being an adult."

Jordy had stared at her incredulously. "You standing up for him?"

"Nobody does *everything* wrong."

Those words came back to her now as she stared at the pill counter. Of all the things this man might be in life, that was one she never would have guessed at if she didn't already know. Because despite the weariness in his eyes, he was the most intense man she'd ever seen, and in her former life she'd seen some prime examples.

And she wasn't sure she liked that intensity being turned on her.

Sexy girl rocker….

How could she be so flattered and so irritated at him at the same time? Perhaps it was the way he'd said it, so casually, as if it were self-evident. And he couldn't know he was hitting a nerve.

A nerve that made her say, rather sharply, "Your wife has a kid and you never knew? How did that work?"

"She…wasn't my wife. Then."

Kai considered this, puzzled over it, and the only answer that fit was that he'd married her after he found out about Jordy. The boy hadn't mentioned it, only that he'd never known his father, and wished his mother had never married him. She'd assumed he'd walked out on them, which had given her even more reason not to like the man.

Seven months, he'd said.

Jordy's mother, he'd told her, died six months ago.

Which meant Wyatt Blake married her knowing she was dying.

Or perhaps because?

This put a whole new light on things for her. Whatever else his sins were, and according to

Jordy they were many, Wyatt Blake was obviously trying to do the right thing by his son. The concern that had driven him here was apparently real, and somehow knowing that made his rude, accusatory questions easier to stomach. No less annoying, but slightly less temper-provoking.

"Look, Mr. Blake," she began, "Jordy's having a tough time. He misses the place he knew, his friends…."

"Those *friends* he misses are why we're here. He was headed down a bad road."

"At thirteen?"

"You think there's an age limit? You of all people should know better."

She bristled anew, her kinder thoughts about him forgotten. "Me, of all people?"

He jerked a thumb toward the photograph. "Half the kids in that audience were probably high."

That hit a little too close to a nerve that would never heal, and she didn't want to talk about it, especially not to this man who seemed intent on his interrogation and entirely oblivious of her efforts to be reasonable.

"What exactly do you want, Mr. Blake? I told you your son is here and what he's doing. If you're afraid of him falling under my evil sway, you can order him not to come back. But I'll tell you up front that you'll regret it."

His brows lowered, and he looked even more intense. And, she admitted, intimidating. But she stood her ground, even when he said in a voice that sent a chill through her, "Is that a threat?"

"That," she said determinedly, "is a simple fact. Playing is the one thing, the only thing, Jordy likes in his life right now. You take it away from him, give him no solace for what's been done to him, and you'll lose him completely."

"Done to him? I brought him here to keep him out of some serious trouble. He was hanging with some kids who were headed that way fast."

"Fine. But he's in no danger here. Contrary to what you think."

"Why should I believe you?"

Exasperation crowded out the wariness his voice had roused in her. "Why shouldn't you?

Or do you approach everyone you don't even know with the assumption they're lying?"

For an instant she saw something that looked like surprise cross his face. Then, in a voice she found, perhaps oddly, incredibly sad, he gave her an equally sad answer. "Yes."

Again she got that impression of utter and total exhaustion. Not so much physical, he looked too fit and leanly muscled for that, but mentally. And emotionally, if she was willing to admit he might have any emotions other than anger, which she wasn't. She—

Her thoughts broke off as Jordy emerged from the soundproof room. The boy stopped dead when he spotted his father.

"What are you doing here?"

The words held a barely suppressed anger tinged with a hurt it took a moment for Kai to figure out. Then she realized this had been Jordy's safe place, the one place his father hadn't known about and therefore didn't intrude upon. And now that was gone, and, judging by his expression, he felt he had nothing left that was his.

"Looking for you. So you can explain why you lied about studying after school."

Jordy flushed. "I lied to keep you off my back."

"Yet here I am. Again. Go get in the car."

Something in his words made Kai remember Jordy's story about the times he'd run away after they'd first come here, and how his father always seemed to find him and drag him back, no matter how hard he tried to hide where he'd gone. That had to mean he cared, didn't it? Or did it mean Jordy was right, that his father only wanted him so he could push him around?

When Jordy had first started coming here—after the third futile effort to run away—she'd wondered, enough that she kept a close eye on the boy for any sign of abuse. Finally she'd asked him, and Jordy's surprise, then grudging admittance that his father had never struck him, told her it was the truth.

"He put a fist through a wall once, though," Jordy had said, as if he felt he needed to prove to her that his father was as bad as he'd been saying.

"Better than backhanding you in the face,"

she'd pointed out, and Jordy had subsided. She
wasn't so far removed from her own teenage
years that she didn't remember what a pain she
herself had been, and sometimes she wondered
why her own father hadn't slapped her silly a
time or two.

So she empathized with Jordy, tremendously.
But now that Wyatt Blake was standing here,
looking at the boy who looked so much like
him with such frustration, she found herself
empathizing with him as well. Not because
of the frustration, but because beneath it she
thought she saw something else.

Fear.

Whether it was fear of failing at the job he
thought he sucked at, or of what would happen
to Jordy if he did fail, she didn't know. But
either way, she knew that deep down this man
did care.

"My mom was so wrong," Jordy said. "She
always told me you were a hero. But you're not
and I hate you."

His father just took it. He never even reacted,
and Kai guessed he'd heard it all before. His
flat "I know" tugged at something deep inside

her. Moved by that unexpected emotion, and remembering what Marilyn had said earlier, she spoke as if Jordy hadn't said any of it.

"So, were you glad to come back home?" she asked.

The man frowned as he looked at her.

"Me?" he finally asked, with such an undertone of puzzlement that she wondered if he'd spent any time at all dealing with his own feelings since he'd apparently taken Jordy on.

"You," she said, keeping an eye on Jordy, who was still glaring at his father. "You moved from wherever you were living, too."

"No," his father said. "I wasn't glad. I never wanted to come back here."

She saw a flicker of surprise cross the boy's face. He'd obviously never thought of this. Perhaps never thought about his father having feelings at all. But he quickly recovered, the sullen expression taking over again.

"And you never wanted me, either."

Again his father didn't react to the fierce declaration.

"Get in the car, Jordan," he said. "You've got homework to do."

Jordan opened his mouth, and for an instant Kai held her breath, thinking Jordy might earn that backhand with the words she could almost feel rising to his lips. But the boy conquered the urge, and after a long glare at his father he stalked toward the door. She saw Blake pull a set of keys out of his jeans pocket, aim one toward the glass door and hit the unlock button. The lights on a black SUV parked just to the right of the shop entrance flashed. He watched the boy open the door and climb into the passenger seat.

"He walks here from school, you know. He could walk home," she said.

"Not safe," he said, almost absently, still focused on the car.

"In Deer Creek?"

"Anywhere."

He muttered it, so low she could barely hear it. And then he turned back to look at her. The key was still in his hand, and she saw his fingers move over it.

"Wishing you could lock him in it?" she asked. "Maybe until he's eighteen?"

His head snapped around. She felt that assessing gaze once more, as if he were gauging if she'd been joking or seriously accusing.

"Thirty," he said after a moment, apparently going with the former.

That was progress, she supposed. And she couldn't help smiling widely at the so normal, parental answer. "Now you sound like *my* father."

He seemed to pull back a little. His gaze flicked once more to the photograph of her on the wall. "He probably still wishes he had kept you locked up until you were thirty."

So much for progress, she thought. "You get scorned by a girl in a band once, or what?"

"Can't imagine any father wanting that life for his daughter."

Her father had, in fact, expressed his concerns. On occasion, strongly. But he'd done it gently, out of love, not out of…whatever it was driving Wyatt Blake to snipe at her.

Which drove her to say, very, very sweetly, "Oh, no. Much better that she live a nice, normal life, maybe fall for some guy who takes what he wants then walks blithely away, not even bothering to find out if she might be pregnant."

The hit scored, and by his expression it was a good one. Which, she supposed, told her a little more about this man; if he was a complete jerk he wouldn't be feeling anything.

But then, if he were that jerk, he wouldn't have bothered to take Jordy, would he? She fought back a growing curiosity about how it had all happened. Why she was feeling that at all was beyond her, after the way he'd talked to her. His concern for his son excused a lot, but to come in here, into her own place, and talk to her like that, was beyond infuriating.

"So are we done?" she asked, letting her feelings show completely this time, now that Jordy was safely out of earshot.

"No."

Startled, she drew back slightly.

"You're going to forbid him to come here? Take that away from him, too?"

He ignored that. "I hear there are some guys who hang out here, guys I don't want my son around."

"Bands practice in my sound room. A lot of

guys—and girls, thank you—hang out. Would you rather have them maybe going somewhere they could find some real trouble?"

What you'll drive Jordy to if you're not careful, she added inwardly.

Again, he ignored her point. "These aren't musicians of any stripe. Where this kind hangs out, there's trouble, eventually."

Although she admitted silently that there were a couple of customers she could do without, exasperation prodded her to say, "Even the cops have to wait until somebody *does* something to convict them."

Something flashed through his eyes then, something dark and grim, and her breath caught. "Thankfully I'm not a cop. I don't have to wait."

Still unsettled by that look, Kai changed her tactics. "There's no one who causes trouble in my store," she said, then added pointedly, "so I keep my nose out of their business."

"Watch they don't get their hands—or worse—in yours," he said. His tone was as grim as that expression had been, and she of the usually quick comeback couldn't think of a thing to say.

And then he was gone, turning on his heel and heading for the vehicle where his son sat waiting in a full-blown sulk.

If it wasn't for the fact that everything she'd said about Jordy coming here was true, she almost wished he really would forbid the boy's visits. At least then she'd be a lot more likely to never have to speak to his father again. And that was a win on her scale.

Chapter 4

The battles, for today at least, were over.

Wyatt sat wearily in the leather chair beside the now dark reading lamp. After Jordan had gone to bed he'd made a circuit of the house, then the big yard, inspecting every step of the way, looking for any sign those "old acquaintances" had overcome those misdirections and found him anyway.

If it was just him, he'd take his chances, rely on the skills that, while perhaps a bit rusty, he knew were still there, waiting. But now there was Jordan, and that changed everything. He couldn't even risk assuming his old colleague was right, that the person asking about him was a friendly. Or if he had been, that he still was.

Again relying on that compartmentalization, he had finished the paperwork and reports for work, details he was allowed to complete at home, which in turn allowed him to be here almost all the hours Jordan wasn't in school. His generous boss had two kids of his own, and although they were adults now, he remembered the teenage years well enough to be sympathetic with Wyatt's predicament.

And you should be with his, Wyatt told himself, thinking of the suspicious incidents that had been occurring at the plant—evidence of a prowler, footprints, broken shrubbery, movement seen by the young night watchman. But the property surrounding the plant was open forest, with free access, so it was hard to prove it was even connected to the plant.

But he knew it was. He also knew he was lucky just to have the job he had. He'd hesitated to approach John Hunt, not liking the idea of cashing in on the sincere but emotion-driven "I owe you everything. If there's ever anything I can do," that the man had delivered years ago. He'd anticipated feeling like a beggar, or worse.

But John had been there like some—too many—of his former bosses never had been. He'd understood immediately, offered him a couple of jobs he knew he didn't want before they had, reluctantly on John's part, settled on the inventory control position the man couldn't believe he really wanted.

"I need to learn how not to think," he said, wanting to be honest about his reasons even as he realized that was the last thing he probably should have said to a prospective employer.

John Hunt had studied him for a long moment. The man was smart, you didn't build the kind of thriving enterprise he had built if you were stupid or lazy. Hunt Packing—affectionately known by its employees as "Little HP," as opposed to the computer giant—was small, but a model of success in a difficult time.

"You can have whatever job you want, Wyatt," he'd finally said. "If you promise that when the time comes that you want more, you'll come to me."

He doubted that time would ever come. He'd had enough, he didn't want challenge. He wanted numbness. No more life-altering decisions, no more explosive situations.

The thought of things explosive brought back what he'd been trying to avoid thinking about all evening; his abrasive encounter with the high-spirited and strong-willed proprietor of Play On. If stereotypes held a kernel of truth, then she lived up to the hair.

And she'd been more restrained than many would have been under the circumstances. He'd come in firing, and looking back, he wouldn't have blamed her if she'd thrown him out, or called those cops. Of course, if she was up to something nefarious that drew those kids he was trying to keep Jordan away from, it wasn't likely she'd be calling the cops for anything.

It occurred to him he should do some homework of his own, something he should have done before he'd charged into Play On. He supposed it was a measure of his progress in the last year that what would have been second nature in the past had only occurred to him so belatedly.

He didn't want to move, had been seriously considering trying to sleep right here in this chair. But he also knew he didn't dare risk Jordan finding out he was checking up on his girl idol, so he'd better do it now.

He got up wearily and walked to the desk in the den. He hadn't powered the computer down after he'd finished his work, so a touch on the mouse brought it back to life.

He began to build the picture.

She was a couple of months shy of thirty. She'd seemed younger to him, but everyone did lately. Born in the heartland, although her parents, solid, level-headed folks, had moved to the West Coast early on in her life. Ordinary childhood, it seemed. She'd been listed as a flower girl in two family weddings before she was five. Then nothing until some speculation in middle school, after a district tournament in which she had apparently smoked the competition, that she might have a future playing tennis. That surprised him; how did you go from potential tennis player to a rock band?

He found the answer in a quote from her, upon the release of Relative Fusion's first CD.

"Tennis didn't make my blood sing," she'd said. "Music does."

The history of the band was easy enough to trace; there were those who still mourned the end even now, years later. They were praised for deep songwriting, the powerful voice of lead singer Christopher "Kit" Hudson, and the innovative arrangements and playing credited to Kai Reynolds. Some canny internet promotion, also credited to Reynolds, plus rabidly loyal fans who adored their "Kit and Kai"—a bit cute, he thought—had brought them to the attention of a small, independent label. Their first CD release had done well enough to encourage a bigger sales campaign on the second.

"Kai's the brains," one label representative was quoted as saying. "She's got a knack for the business. If she ever quits performing, we'd hire her in a minute."

So perhaps it wasn't such a reach that she'd ended up running a small-town music store, that she'd gone from winding up venues full of appreciative fans to selling instruments to the local high school band program.

From electric guitars to tubas, he thought wryly.

But she hadn't, by all accounts, wanted to quit performing. It had been taken out of her hands. One writer, on a popular blog chronicling the music scene in the Northwest, had told the story in bleak detail; the death of lead singer Kit Hudson, and the resulting departure of lead guitarist Kai Reynolds, had spelled the end for the inventive, talented and rising band.

"The fiery couple were the nucleus of Relative Fusion," the man wrote. "Onstage and off. When Hudson died tragically of an accidental overdose at twenty-six, it took the heart, and the music, out of Reynolds, and she quit the band shortly thereafter. Without that nucleus the rest of the band disintegrated quickly, going their separate ways."

...took the heart, and the music, out of Reynolds.

It only took a couple of minutes to find what apparently was the only public statement she'd ever made on her lover's death.

"Kit's death is the biggest waste I'm ever likely to see in my life. I loved him, but he wouldn't, couldn't stop. I can't be a part of a world that will remind me every day that he was just the latest in a long line that will continue endlessly."

He read the words again, and then a third time. Including the reference at the bottom of the article that as Hudson's executor, she had funneled his entire take from the music into funding a rehab clinic in his hometown.

He could almost feel his view of her shift. And he suddenly doubted she was either doing, enabling or selling drugs in the back of her store.

The blogger may have been right, death may have taken the heart out of her, but she had also apparently seen it for what it was, another in a long line of deaths chalked up to not just the drugs but their prevalence in her world.

So she'd walked away.

She'd left behind a career she probably loved, doing what kids all over the world dreamed of doing, and having achieved some amount of success at it. She probably could have stayed; played with another band, but she'd left before it swallowed her up, too.

And he found himself admiring her for having the wisdom and courage to walk away from a soul-eating existence.

And to do it a lot sooner than he had.

Kai knew who it was the moment she heard the back door open. Only one person came in that way when there was still parking out front. She wasn't sure why, or why it faintly annoyed her.

"Hello, Max."

"Hey, sweet thing."

She tried not to wince at the overdone effort at charm. Max was barely into his twenties, fairly good-looking with thick, medium-brown hair, flashing dark eyes and a killer grin, but he walked and talked with a smug swagger she instinctively disliked. She'd seen it before, and in her experience there was rarely anything of substance beneath all the bravado.

But at least he was alone, this time. When he came in with his two followers, he was a different guy, the bravado taking on an ugly edge. Part of maintaining his leadership in his small posse, she supposed. But whatever it was, she didn't like it, and she was wary whenever the three of them came in together.

And he was a customer, a regular one. Not for instruments; he spent his time in either the sound system corner, or the small CD section in the opposite corner of the store. The big box store in the next town drew people for the big sellers, so she focused on the stuff they didn't, the smaller, local groups, Americana, the indies, alternative and the more eclectic, off-the-beaten-path stuff. Things it was hard to find even to download, not in any coherent manner. It didn't make a huge profit, but most quarters she broke even on it. And since he was a not-insignificant contributor to that, she kept wearing her best service-oriented smile.

But today he wasn't looking at CDs; instead he leaned forward and rested his elbows on the counter.

"Remember that sound system we were talking about?"

"I think we were drooling more than talking, but yes," she said, her smile more genuine as she remembered Max's very real enthusiasm for the very expensive equipment.

Max laughed, and he seemed to drop the swagger. "I want it," he said.

"Don't we all. You could blast music all the way to Seattle."

"No, I mean I want to order them."

She blinked. "The price hasn't changed in two weeks, Max."

"I know. But my…resources have."

"You get a nine-to-five?" she asked wryly.

"Shit, no," Max exclaimed with a grin. "I'm a freelancer, you know that. The everyday grind, that's for drones, you know? Worker bees."

Like your parents, she thought; the Middletons were a hardworking pair, but they were anything but wealthy. And Max still lived with them, Kai suspected because he had them charmed—or buffaloed—into continuing to support him, negating the necessity for him to actually do something with his young life.

"Don't tell me you talked your dad into springing for expensive, high-end speaker gear so you can blow him out of his own home?"

He laughed again, but there was an edge in it this time, as if something she'd said had rubbed his pride the wrong way.

"Nah," he said. "But he's giving me the garage. I'm going to convert it into the biggest, baddest entertainment room in this whole loser little town."

Kai had the thought that if the latter was really true, accomplishing the former wouldn't take much, but kept it to herself.

"So, you gonna order those bad boys for me?"

"Look, Max," she said frankly, "I can't afford to eat the cost of an order that big. You sure you can manage it?"

She'd been afraid he would take offense— funny how those with the least reason got their egos in a pucker the easiest—but instead he reacted as if he'd only been waiting for her to ask. With dramatic flair he reached into his jacket pocket and pulled out a wad of cash.

"Sure, I can. I'll even pay the whole thing in advance," he said with a smile that told her she was supposed to be impressed.

"Cash?" she said, surprised.

"I've been saving up. Doing some favors for a friend," he said, with a pious look she couldn't help doubting. "He's very grateful."

He was counting it out as he laid it out on the

counter, mostly tens and twenties but the occasional fifty and even a couple of Benjamins.

"You're sure about this?" she asked, wondering what was wrong with her, why she didn't just leap at the sale. It would put her well into the black for the month, and lessen the worry about the next month as well. And he could have easily just ordered them online, or gone out of town to one of the big electronic or audio/video stores that would have what he wanted, maybe even in stock. But he'd come here, and she should, she told herself, be more appreciative.

Even if she suspected he had more in mind than just a proprietor-customer relationship.

"There's more where this came from," he answered. "There's always more." He flashed that smile at her again. "I'm even paying my old man rent, how about that?"

Well, that's something, Kai thought, and pulled out a form to make the order. She made a call, found out the equipment was available for immediate shipment. When she had all the information, she marked down the amount paid, and signed the receipt.

"Hey, look at that, I finally got your auto-graph!"

She couldn't help laughing at that. "I'll call you when they come in. Shouldn't be more than a couple of days."

"And don't forget the phone number after," he said, with what she supposed was his best effort at a leer.

Max was always flirting with her, in a clumsy way she found odd and somewhat amusing, a reaction she guessed he wouldn't be too happy about.

Today's riff, a Stephen Bruton favorite, sounded again. She looked over, and was re-lieved to see Jordy coming in. Apparently his father had decided against forbidding the boy to come here.

Or he had, and Jordy was disobeying.

She hoped it wasn't that. Not only for Jordy's sake but her own; she so did not want to be in the middle of that mess, with Wyatt Blake coming after her again, the way he had last week. She'd be happy never to see the man again.

But somehow she didn't think she was going to be that lucky.

* * *

"You wanted to see me, sir?"

John Hunt looked up and motioned Wyatt into the office.

"Close the door, will you?"

Uh-oh.

Wyatt did as asked, but warily. John was normally the most approachable of bosses, genial and willing to listen, hence the usually open door.

He stopped in front of the man's desk, shaking his head at the offer of a seat; he hoped he wasn't going to be there that long. Hoped as well this was just to catch up after the man's recent business trip. Doubted he was that lucky.

"I meant to tell you this before I left for the East Coast, but I'm afraid it slipped my mind. I'm still not sure if it means anything, but it might to you."

Truly wary now, Wyatt asked, "What?"

"About a week before I left I got a phone call about you."

Wyatt went very still. "A phone call?"

"From somebody else who owes you."

"That's what they said?"

John nodded. "They thought I might know where you were."

A week before. And John had been gone two weeks. He could have been already burned three weeks ago. His mind was racing as John studied him.

"I told him I didn't. Just like you asked."

"Thank you."

For all the good it would do. If whoever it was knew enough to call here, then he could find him. John was the only one who knew about his desire for secrecy; they'd decided early on it would make things worse rather than better if they asked everybody at Hunt Packing to keep him secret. Better just to give them nothing to talk about.

But that didn't help if you had people calling and asking about him directly.

And back then, it had been merely a precaution. Now, this coupled with that emailed warning….

"Wyatt—"

His boss stopped when he shook his head. And let him go.

Wyatt headed back to his cubicle. When he'd

gotten tangled up in the mess John's youngest daughter had gotten herself into, he'd been startled to learn the man's business was headquartered so close to his old hometown. And been thankful she'd gone off to the big city to get herself in trouble; he'd been nowhere near ready to go home, for any reason.

And now here he was, back again, hiding. Trying to keep his son out of the same kind of mess.

Only now he was wondering if his own less-than-tidy past was going to follow them here.

Wondering if anybody ever got to truly leave their past behind them.

Chapter 5

"Hey, kid," Max said to Jordy.

"Hi, Max!"

The boy seemed thrilled that the older boy—Kai couldn't think of Max any other way—had acknowledged him. Did more than just acknowledge him, even gave him a friendly, man-to-man-type slap on the shoulder.

"Been practicing?" Max asked as Kai brought out the boxes containing his speakers and added them to the stack.

Jordy lit up at Max's attention. "Yeah! Kai let me play BeeGee the other day."

"Miss Kai," Max said with a fair approximation of Old World charm, "is a generous soul."

"She's the best," Jordy said, so fervently it made Kai smile.

"Thank you, Jordy," she said.

"Gonna play in a band someday, like she did?" Max asked, with every evidence of genuine interest in this boy at least ten years younger than he. His two buddies treated the boy like most guys their age would, with annoyance bordering on anger, but a few weeks ago Max had changed, started being nice to Jordy, at least around her.

But it seemed different to her today.

I hear there are some guys who hang out here, guys I don't want my son around....

Wyatt Blake, that was the difference. He'd unsettled her, made her suspicious.

Even as she thought it, watching the two males talk as if they were of an age, she knew that wasn't quite true. Because it was odd that Max had started to show up mostly in the afternoons, around the time Jordy always came in. Odder still that someone Max's age, unless he was a relative, would even pretend such an interest in a kid so much younger. And she'd thought that even before Jordy's father had come barreling into her life.

So why hadn't she told him? Why hadn't she aimed him at Max, let him be the one to ferret out the true reason behind this unexpected kindness by someone who was, from what she'd heard outside the store, generally surly and rude most of the rest of the time?

Because Wyatt Blake aggravated you?

Because he *had* aggravated her. He had provoked the temper she'd worked hard to quash. She'd worked hard at it because she hated being a cliché, a redhead with a hot temper. And she'd managed to put a respectably long fuse on it, and then hide the matches, after years of effort.

She hadn't counted on a guy who brought his own lighter.

She yanked herself out of unwelcome thoughts.

"Your old man still giving you a hard time?" Max was asking.

Jordy shot her a quick, sideways glance. "It never stops. Ask Kai. He was in here hassling her last week."

Max looked at her, his pierced right brow lifting. She shrugged. "He was here. But I can't blame him for wanting to know where his son spends a lot of time."

Jordy's eyes widened, she supposed at the unexpected defense of the man he hated. "He was a jerk!"

There was the tiniest hint of a hovering sense of betrayal in the words, so Kai grinned at the boy and said, "I believe I told him that. And worse."

In an instant Jordy's mood shifted. "You did?" he asked, wide-eyed and with an awed tone.

"I did. You can't, but I can, because he can't do anything to me," she said.

"Parents. Always trying to run your life," Max put in.

She focused on the older boy for a moment. "When you're only thirteen, that's the way it is," she said, watching Max's face for any sense of surprise at how young Jordy really was. There was no reaction, and she knew he'd already known. Which made his amiability toward the boy who was barely more than a child even more suspect.

"I can't wait until I'm eighteen," Jordy said. "I'll take off and never come back."

Kai thought about pointing out that some kids stayed and leeched off their parents into their twenties, but decided poking at Max wasn't the best path right now. After all, she had nothing to indicate the guy was really a problem, nothing suspicious except the way he treated a much younger boy, and the ready cash with no visible source. His rather awkward but harmless flirting with her, and his kindness and interest in Jordy might be out of character, but hardly a crime.

The money? Maybe he really had done favors for a friend.

And maybe you're the queen of gullibleville, she told herself drily.

She remembered her thoughts later as, walking back from the grocery store to her apartment over the store, she saw Max and his two regular companions standing outside the local pizza place a block down off the main street, across from the bakery. Most of the local teenagers hung out at Dinozzo's, and since Max and his friends didn't seem to have progressed beyond that age, she supposed it was reasonable that they would, too.

She glanced down the street again as she crossed at the corner. There was a row of outdoor tables with umbrellas, lit by lights on the outside of the building. They'd be put away for the winter soon, and the lights dimmed, but for now the area in front was lit like a stage. Just as she reached the opposite curb, she saw Dan, the least likeable of Max's two regular companions, gesture to an older man around the corner of the building.

She kept walking.

Forget it, she told herself. Just get home. It's late, you're starved, and it's affecting your imagination.

She fired up her barbecue before she put the groceries away, then quickly fixed a salad and put the steak she'd bought on the grill out on her small back balcony, big enough only for the barbecue and a pub-style table with a couple of stools. She liked the high seating because it allowed her to look over the railing and across the small neighborhood that was dotted with so many trees it made for a pleasantly green landscape. In the distance were the mountains, and the vista gave her a feeling of space that was an antidote to the cramped balcony.

Not that her apartment itself was cramped, it was as big as the store below, and two years ago she'd had it remodeled so that the walled off kitchen was now open to the main living area in a great room effect. And she liked it.

"You'll be bored to tears in that little town," her mother had warned her.

But for once, her mother had been wrong. She loved it, she loved living here, loved her store, all of it. And despite the confidence she'd expressed all along to her parents, no one had been more surprised than she was that Kai Reynolds was actually a small-town girl at heart.

She decided to eat outside; it would soon be too chilly, and she'd miss the opportunity. For the first few bites she focused on how good the local beef was, and the tang of Mrs. Bain's homemade salad dressing, well worth the regular trips to the weekend farmer's market. She'd have to stock up for the winter soon, before the markets ended for the season. She didn't go for

any esoteric, organic reasons, but simply because she liked the feel of it, the way things
used to be in a simpler time.

A simpler time. A simpler place.

She thought of what she'd seen by the pizza
parlor, Max and his friends, which led her to
Jordy. Could she really blame his father for
bringing him here when she herself had come
here seeking many of the same things? Could
she blame him for making assumptions when
in a great many stores like hers what he'd ac-
cused her of—the paraphernalia at least—was
in fact true? Had she been so predisposed because of Jordy's complaints that she hadn't
given the man a chance?

She played the encounter back in her mind.
No, he was pretty much a jerk from the beginning. But, she admitted, she'd made no effort
to be conciliatory, either. She'd gone on offense
from the moment he'd opened his mouth, reacting to his harsh tone more than what he'd said.
And it had gone downhill from there.

She was still pondering when she went to
bed. Maybe she should have told him about
Max. At least that Jordy was fascinated by the

older boys, and the attention Max in particular paid him, enough that Kai was wary. Maybe she still should. After all, his father was only trying to keep the boy out of trouble.

"Or maybe you should just stay butted out," she muttered into the darkness.

She was certainly no expert on raising kids, her only experience stemming from the kid side. But by his own admission, neither was Jordy's father.

I should call Mom, she thought again. *Ask her how she liked getting parenting advice from strangers who weren't even parents themselves. That ought to cure the urge.*

She rolled over and pounded her pillow into submission. When it didn't seem to help, when sleep seemed no closer, she sighed aloud.

Damn Wyatt Blake anyway. Wasn't it enough that he soaked up all the air in the room in person, did he have to invade her thoughts, too?

Apparently so, she thought, humor sparking at last, since she'd been thinking about that rancorous encounter for nearly a week now.

...only trying to keep the boy out of trouble.

She lifted herself up on an elbow, remembering Jordy saying with all his thirteen-year-old determination, "He wants me to do sports or something, and I won't. I don't want to do *anything* he says."

An idea stirred. She lay there, considering, turning it over and around in her mind.

It might work, she thought. It just might work.

And if it didn't, they'd be right where they were now, except Jordy's father would likely be even angrier at her.

But at least this time she would have done something to deserve it. Meddling, her mother would call it.

But then, her mother had also said that sometimes meddling wasn't all bad.

Decided now, she put her head back down on the pillow. And sleep, as if it had been waiting for a decision, came quickly.

Chapter 6

Saturday morning dawned clear and crisp. Good for a walk, Kai told herself. It would soon be time to break out her beloved shearling jacket and boots, and that made her smile. Maybe she'd learn to knit this winter, so she could make some of those cool beanies and watch caps she loved.

So, she thought, I'm in such a good mood, what better to do than destroy it?

She grabbed the DVD that was the pretext she'd come up with, and trotted downstairs. She pulled on the medium-weight jacket that hung by the back door, stuffed the DVD case in the pocket and stepped outside. She locked up behind her and started west. From Jordy she knew they were living in his grandparent's old home at the far end of Madrona Street, and that they were both dead. That fact was meaningless to Jordy, since he'd never known his father, let alone his father's parents.

It was only about a half a mile, nice for a walk on a brisk fall day. She'd have time to get there and back, since she didn't open the store until noon on Saturdays. And since it was in an area she hadn't perused much, she was looking forward to it. The walk part, anyway.

She hummed under her breath as she went, pleased that it didn't bother her overmuch when she realized it was the last song Kit had written. She smiled and waved at people who went by if she knew them, leaving it at a smile if she didn't. She did a lot of waving. She'd gone out of her way to meet as many people as she could when she'd come here, not just for business reasons. She'd had some idea in her head that the small town might close ranks against the outsider. But instead they'd welcomed her, been thrilled that their little town was going to have a music store, and she'd slid into a comfortable place here more quickly than she'd ever imagined possible.

So, was she about to mess with that, too? Wyatt Blake was one of their own; after all, he'd grown up here. Would they suddenly decide she was an interloper if she started interfering in his life?

She shook her head, nearly laughing out loud at herself. If that's all it took, then her place here wasn't as comfortable as she thought it was.

She glanced at her watch, saw that it was after nine now. Her mom liked to sleep in on Sundays, and given the dynamo she was the rest of the week, no one was likely to argue with her. She pulled out her cell phone and made the call she'd been meaning to make for days now.

Her mother never chided her for not calling often enough, which actually made her call more often than her busy life conveniently allowed. Her mother, Kai thought for at least the millionth time, was a very smart woman.

After the usual catching up, and the pleasant news that her father was feeling so much better after knee surgery a few months ago that he'd gone fishing with some friends, Kai asked the question she'd been pondering.

"Do you think someone who's never had kids can ever have good ideas about raising them?"

"Of course," her mother said, "if they ever were one."

Kai laughed. "Did anybody who'd never had them ever tell you what you should do with me?"

"I seem to recall your Uncle Brad having an opinion or two on the matter."

She laughed again at her mother's dry tone; her Uncle Brad Reynolds, her father's brother, made Wyatt Blake look like an overly lenient pushover.

"I always had the feeling Uncle Brad thought kids shouldn't just be seen and not heard, they shouldn't *be*."

"He would be much more comfortable with them if they were born adults," her mother agreed.

"Thanks for keeping him at a distance for me."

"In my job description," her mother said

with a laugh. "Now, you want to tell me what brought this on?"

"Just a kid who's been hanging around the store. He's having trouble with his dad."

"And you think dad's the problem?"

"I've met him," Kai said. "Yeah, I think he's the problem."

"Thinking of meddling?"

"On my way to do it right now," Kai admitted. "He's a good kid. I'm worried about him."

"Then that's your approach. No parent who really cares wouldn't at least listen to someone who starts out saying they're worried about their child."

"You haven't met this one," Kai said. "But I'll give that a shot. Thanks, Mom."

She tucked the phone back into her pocket and made the turn onto Madrona Street. The road ended down where there were older houses, houses with large yards and classic, Craftsman-style architecture she admired. But Jordy hated the house, too, and talked about being at the end of the street like it was the end of the world.

She found the house, two stories of perfect

details, sitting back from the cul de sac on a large lot. So that was the huge lawn Jordy griped about having to mow, she thought. She could see his point, it was pretty big. But at least he'd get the winter off; hard to mow when it was raining nearly every day.

And it looked good, she thought as she started up the gently winding walkway that was a nice counterpoint to the squares and rectangles of the house and driveway. She wondered if Jordy did that good a job by nature, or only because he knew his father would make him do it over again if it was too sloppy. She kind of leaned toward the latter, from what she'd seen and heard.

She was at the porch, contemplating the cowardly act of just leaving the DVD and hoping Jordy's father would get the hint, when the meaning of the rhythmic sounds she'd been hearing registered. Somebody was chopping wood.

Surely not Jordy? He was too small to be using an ax, at least a full-size one, safely. She walked toward the noise, around the corner of the house. And stopped dead.

In the shade of a huge tree next to the house, Wyatt Blake was doing the woodman routine. And doing it well, with the same grace and power she'd sensed in him the first moment she'd seen him.

And he was doing it in jeans and a worn T-shirt despite the coolness of the morning. But she guessed nothing worked up a sweat like chopping wood.

For a long moment she just stood there, watching the man work with a sort of fascination she didn't understand. She was no expert on the procedure, but it certainly seemed he was; he had a smooth rhythm going that was seamless, even as it adapted to different sizes of the logs he was splitting into fireplace-size chunks.

Okay, so she liked the way he moved. Liked the lean, rangy way he was built. She could appreciate that, right?

She wondered anew if this was perhaps one of her less brilliant ideas, if she should have gone with the urge to leave the DVD and vanish.

And then it was out of her hands; she hadn't

even noticed Jordy was there, dutifully if sullenly stacking the split lengths of wood his father was producing at a rather amazing rate. But the boy spotted her in the moment before she could turn coward and run.

"Kai!"

Delight spread across his face as he dropped the wood he held and trotted toward her, making it impossible for her to flee. The rhythmic sounds of the striking ax stopped abruptly, then a louder strike sounded as Jordy's father buried the head of the ax deeply into the tree stump he'd been using as a chopping block. For a moment she met his eyes, saw that cool assessment again, that expressionless mask.

With an inward sigh, she steeled herself. She turned back to Jordy as the boy asked excitedly, "What are you doing here?"

She saw, from the corner of her eye, Jordy's father had left the chopping block and was walking toward them, and she had the feeling those were the words in his mind as well, although likely in a much less welcoming tone.

She kept her focus on the boy. "I brought you something," she said.

Jordy's eyes widened. "Me? You brought me something?"

He sounded so astonished that her heart ached a little.

"Yes, you." She tugged the jewel case out of her jacket pocket. "Remember, we talked about that teaching DVD?"

Jordy's eyes lit up. "You found it?"

"Yep."

His father was there now, just a yard or so away. But he didn't speak at all, didn't interrupt, so she kept her eyes on the boy.

"Now, this is the only copy I have, and it's out of production now, so you need to be careful with it. But the guy who did it is a great teacher, I think you'll like him."

"And he's really the guy who taught you to play?"

"He's the guy who took my playing from plinking around to actually sounding like something, yes."

"Cool!"

Jordy's enthusiasm was infectious, and she grinned at him. "Let's see how you feel when your fingers start bleeding."

Jordy's grin started strong, but faded. "But I'll need to practice, won't I?"

"A lot."

He cast a sideways glance at his father, his expression going from delight to anger and dislike. "But I can't."

Jordy didn't say "He won't let me," but the inference was clear.

"Why don't you take that inside," she told the boy. "Let me talk to your dad for a minute."

For an instant hope flared in those eyes so like yet unlike his father's. Then it was gone, although he took the DVD and headed toward the house. Defeat screamed from him with every trudging step, and she couldn't stop herself from turning back to the man standing there. He looked exasperated.

"Didn't even argue," he muttered.

"You're crushing him."

She regretted the words the moment they came out. She sensed his edgy watchfulness shift into the same mood he'd been under when he'd come into the store last week.

"And you're sticking your nose where it doesn't belong."

"Meddling."

He blinked. "What?"

"My mother calls it meddling."

"She's right," he said, and she couldn't miss the warning note in his voice.

This is for Jordy, she reminded herself.

"I'm sorry," she said. "I didn't mean to start that way. It's just that it breaks my heart to see him like that."

"He's a good whiner."

She drew back slightly, the cold assessment surprising her, although she wasn't sure why it should. "He has things to whine about, don't you think?"

The man pulled off the heavy gloves he'd been wearing and crossed his arms. The body language was clear, but the movement also shifted the sleeve of his shirt, and she caught a glimpse of a wicked, curving scar up the back of his left arm.

"Whining doesn't change anything," he said flatly. "You just have to get on with it."

She tore her gaze from the scar, although the image of it lingered in her mind. She saw in his face that he knew perfectly well she'd seen it, but he wasn't about to explain. No reason he should, she told herself, and spoke only about Jordy.

"So, he's not even allowed to acknowledge his grief, his pain, his fear?"

That made him frown. "Fear?"

"Of course he's afraid. He's just a boy, the one parent he knew and loved is dead, he's never moved before but gets yanked out of the life he knew, away from his friends and anyone he trusted—"

She stopped herself, realizing what she'd just said. But he didn't react, either not taking offense or realizing it was true, Jordy didn't trust him.

"Six months ago," he pointed out.

"One twenty-sixth of his life," she countered. "Not long enough, not when you're so young you don't have the resources to easily adapt. And no one to turn to for help."

"I've tried talking to him. Explaining."

It was the first even slightly conciliatory thing he'd said, and she seized on it.

"He doesn't want to hear it. You can't give him the one thing he wants most. No one can."

"His mother back."

"Yes."

There was a long pause. "She knew I was going to do this. Bring him here. She approved."

"Did she talk to him about it?"

He dropped his arms, slapped the gloves in his right hand against his leg. "She didn't have time."

She studied him for a moment. "You told him she agreed to it?" He nodded. She read what he wasn't saying in those weary eyes. "But he didn't believe you."

"I could tell him the sky is blue and he wouldn't believe me."

She doubted it was quite that bad, but he was talking now, almost reasonably, and she didn't want to waste this chance.

"I know you're worried about him, what kind of trouble he might get into."

"That's why we're here in the first place."

"And he's fighting you."

"Every step of the way."

Like father...

She nearly bit her tongue, afraid the words

that popped into her mind were going to pop out of her mouth. "He doesn't want to do anything you say?"

"I think he only listens so he can do the opposite," he said wryly.

"Then tell him to do the thing he wants most to do."

"Take that ax to me?" he suggested with a jerk of his thumb over his shoulder and a glance toward the chopping block.

It was a bitter, scathing sort of joke, but it was a joke—at least, she thought it was—and she should acknowledge that. But again the movement had tugged at the faded blue T-shirt, and she caught a glimpse of lean, flat stomach.

And another scar on his left side, just above the low-slung waistband of his jeans. This one was tidier, and there were marks from stitches or staples, but also an odd rounded indentation in the middle.

How on earth did a paper pusher—or a pill counter—end up with scars like that? she wondered.

And, almost reluctantly, it occurred to her

that perhaps Wyatt Blake had reason to be the way he was.

It seemed he'd been through his own kind of hell.

Chapter 7

Wyatt saw her gaze snap back to his face as he looked back from the woodpile. She wore the oddest expression on her very expressive face. Not revulsion at his scars, he'd seen that often enough to recognize it. But she wasn't much at hiding her emotions, this one. Did that mean she wasn't much at hiding, period? Was she really what she seemed, just a kind woman who cared about a boy not her own?

They did exist, people like that, he reminded himself. Just because he hadn't run into many for a long time didn't change that. They were the reason he'd chosen the path he'd walked, after all.

"I meant," she said, sounding as if she had been distracted and was trying to regain her focus, "what if you tell him he has to spend every spare minute doing something he actually desperately wants to do? Imagine his dilemma."

He studied her for a moment. "You mean practice playing the guitar."

He thought he saw it now, the motive behind bringing Jordy that instructional DVD.

"Expecting me to buy him a guitar? From your store, of course?"

"I don't care if you build him one from that wood you're chopping," she snapped, startling him.

He shifted uncomfortably as she went on, clearly angry all over again at him.

"I've been loaning him my demo for weeks, and I'll continue to let him use it all he wants. He can even bring it home to practice." She gave him a disgusted look. "No effort at all on your part."

He felt a bit like a man trapped in a burning car with the flames licking at the gas tank.

Time to get the hell out or avert the ensuing explosion.

"Sorry," he muttered, without the grace he supposed was warranted. "I'm just... I don't know what to do with him."

"Like a million other parents."

To her credit, she didn't hang on to her mad. Apparently helping Jordan was more important. And that made him feel more than a little embarrassed at how he'd once again assumed she had base motives.

He let out a compressed breath. "I guess I'm as confused as he is."

As if his admission made up for his accusations, her voice was gentle, encouraging when she said, "Maybe you should tell him that."

"Great way to undermine my authority with him."

"And that's getting you so far, isn't it?"

There wasn't a trace of sarcasm in her voice, but the words stung as if she'd bitten them out in that snapping tone.

"Look," she said, sounding as exasperated with him as he felt with Jordan, "I know I'm not a parent. But I do remember what it was like to be that age. Don't you remember? It was hard. And that was with both parents alive and together. I know yours were."

He stiffened. "You don't know anything about them."

Her brow furrowed. "But Marilyn Ogilvie told me—"

"I can imagine. Tim and Claire Blake, the perfect couple."

"She never said they were perfect. Just that they were good to you, worked hard to give you a good life, and—"

She stopped abruptly, and he nearly laughed. Then he completed the sentence for her.

"And I walked out on them without a word, thankless son that I was."

She was honest enough to admit it. And, he noted, nervy enough to meet his gaze levelly when she did. "Something along those lines, yes."

"I figured that was the line. My father was the proverbial pillar of the community."

He didn't think he sounded anything other

than neutral, observational, but her gaze sharpened.

"But he wasn't the pillar of your family?"

She was, indeed, sharp, he thought.

"More like the walls."

He couldn't quite believe he'd said that; he didn't indulge in esoteric analogies. They wasted time when you had to explain them, and he'd learned young and the hard way the cost of wasted time, a lesson that had been pounded home later.

"Keeping the world at bay?" she asked.

He let out a sigh; this was exactly why—

"No," she said, answering herself, "keeping you in."

He blinked, even after he'd acknowledged her cleverness, startled at how quickly she'd gotten there.

She apparently didn't need to hear him say it, either. "So what did it take to be allowed out?"

"You had to be good enough. I never was. Ever."

He started yanking his work gloves back on, staring at his hands as if the task required the utmost concentration, not quite able to believe he'd said that. Or that he was standing here talking about things he never talked about to a woman he had met exactly once.

That that meeting had stuck in his mind the way little else had in the last year was merely an annoyance.

"So you're going to treat Jordy the same way?"

He stopped in the midst of settling the left glove on his hand. He looked up. She was simply standing there, waiting. And he was standing there, struggling not to admit she had a point. The battle put the sarcasm back in his voice.

"So, Miss 'I know I'm not a parent but,' what do you suggest?"

She didn't respond to his tone, only his words. "That you spend as much time thinking about what to get Jordy involved in as you do about keeping him out of trouble. Because the one will accomplish the other."

For a long, silent moment he stared at her. His thoughts were tumbling, and he needed time to sort them out.

"Excuse me," he said, "but I have work to finish." And thinking to do, he added silently.

"Does nothing else matter? Just work?"

It's all I have, he thought, and gritted his teeth against letting the whiny, pitiful words slip out.

"Let Jordy play," she urged. "A little music in the house can change everything."

"You're saying he's able to produce music?"

Her mouth quirked. "Well, not yet, but he will."

"And in the meantime?"

The quirk became a lopsided smile. "I've got a set of noise-canceling earphones I can loan you."

A short, genuine laugh burst from him, surprising him. She looked almost as surprised as he felt, which told him just how irascible he must seem to her. Yet she'd never given up, she'd confronted him, in essence fighting for what she thought would be good for his son.

With a little shock he realized that for the first time, he felt as if he had some support in this lifetime's work he'd taken on.

The bigger shock was that he welcomed it. Even from a wild-child ex-rocker.

Even though she was only open six hours on Saturday, a great deal of her income was generated on those days when school was out and people were off work. Malmsteen had been breaking the silence fairly steadily, every fifteen or twenty minutes or so, and she made a mental note to make sure she only had something she really, really liked in the rotation for Saturdays.

The riff sounded again on the thought, making her smile as she looked up.

Jordy, she thought in surprise. He was never here on Saturday. Because, he'd once told her, his father had a list of chores for him to do that was so long he wouldn't have time to pee if he did them all. He had immediately blushed, and apologized.

"Sorry, you're a girl, I shouldn't talk about that in front of you."

She'd leaned over and conspiratorially whispered to him, "Guess what? Girls do it, too."

He'd laughed, something rare enough with

him that she'd appreciated it. Something, she guessed, that was even rarer with his father, which would explain why his short laugh earlier this morning had had such an effect on her.

His father, who, she belatedly realized, was now coming through the door. Jordy must have run ahead, she thought.

"Hey, green eyes," she said to the boy as he skidded to a halt at the counter. "What are you doing here on a Saturday?"

"He said I can play! In fact, he said I have to."

Excitement warred with suspicion in his expression, as if he wasn't certain his father wasn't up to something, or wouldn't change his mind, but right now the excitement was winning.

"Excellent," she said, not glancing up at the man she knew perfectly well had come to a halt a few feet away.

"I watched the DVD, even before he said I could come," Jordy said, as if trying to prove his genuine eagerness. "So I already know some stuff to try."

"Next time bring it with you. I'll set up a

player in the sound room so you can watch and work with it."

"Cool!" Then, with a sideways look at her he asked, "But you'll still help me if I get stuck, right?"

"You bet. I'm no teacher, but I can usually see what's going wrong." She gestured toward the back room. "The Strat's already in there. Time's wasting. But only an hour, or you'll make your fingers too sore for next time."

Jordy grinned and wheeled around to head toward the back room.

"Rules."

Jordy stopped in his tracks. It was the first thing Wyatt Blake had said, and Kai couldn't help thinking it seemed typical that it would be that.

"I remember," Jordy said without looking at his father, and darted into the room and closed the door quickly, as if he was afraid the next words from his father would be a retraction of the fragile agreement.

She finally looked at him; he'd showered and changed, his hair was still damp, the jeans less worn out, and the long-sleeved pullover shirt a bit less casual. His jaw also looked freshly shaven, which gave her an odd sort of feeling. Had he done all that just to come here, or just to leave the house in the first place?

"Rules?" she asked.

"He needs them."

Tim was strict, Marilyn Ogilvie had said. "Funny, that's the same thing I heard about you."

He blinked. "What?"

"That you needed rules, reckless as you were."

"Maybe I was reckless," he said, his voice holding an unexpected note of wry humor, "because of all the rules."

She smiled, liking the twist. It was yet another flash of a different man, a man with humor and thoughtfulness, hidden behind the rigid facade.

If it was a facade, she thought, and not the real man through and through, with just a few nicks of real feeling here and there.

"Keep that in mind with your son," she said.

He let out a compressed breath, and looked

away. Had just that mere suggestion shut him down again?

"Anything I need to know? I wouldn't want to be party to him breaking any rules and getting in trouble."

She thought she'd kept any sarcasm out of her words, but when he still didn't look at her, she wondered if some had crept through.

"Just that he's only allowed to come here after school, and only to practice. No hanging out, no wasting homework time."

"Is he allowed to breathe?" she asked, too sweetly. His jaw tightened and she wished she hadn't said it; he had, after all, given in, and she should be nicer to him after that. "Sorry. You're letting him play, that's the big thing."

"I had to do something," he said. Then, rubbing a hand over his eyes as if they felt as tired as they looked, he muttered, "I told you I suck at this."

She chose her next words carefully. "I'm not saying let him do whatever he wants, just…remember how you felt."

He looked up then, and again she had the sense of an incredible weariness dulling the eyes that were alive and vibrant in his son. A sudden rush of compassion filled her.

"It must seem overwhelming," she said softly.

His mouth twisted. "Becoming a father of a teenager at thirty-eight was not on my agenda. I'm trying, but I have no idea how to relate to him, and he won't listen to me anyway."

She couldn't stop herself from doing the math; that meant he'd been twenty-five when Jordy had been born. She stifled the urge to ask him if being a father at all had been on his agenda, not liking that she wanted to know. And liking even less that her first thought had been that he was almost a decade older than she. Chronologically anyway; she had the feeling he was a century older in other ways.

"But he obeys you, mostly, doesn't he?"

"Mostly, yes. Grudgingly."

"So, does any kid do it graciously?" She tried a smile. "Unless it's the month before Christmas or their birthday or something, I mean?"

That earned her a quick, answering smile. And she indeed felt like she'd earned it.

"I just don't want him heading into serious trouble, like he was down in L.A."

"So you keep him so busy he doesn't have time?"

His mouth twisted again, but with that humor this time. "Something like that."

"Works, up to a point. As you know from your own experience, I'm guessing."

"I'm trying to keep him from thinking about his mother too much, too."

"I'm not sure that can be done. I can't imagine losing my mother. I'd be devastated, never the same." Then, curiosity overcoming the need to tread carefully with this man, she added, "You must miss her too."

"I barely knew her."

"Well enough," she said, a bit drily.

To her amazement, he flushed. "Look, it was one time, under…difficult circumstances. We both had our eyes open, we knew what it… wasn't. After, we agreed it would be best to leave it there, and we each went our own way."

"Except she was pregnant," she couldn't help pointing out.

"I never knew. I didn't find out about Jordan until…she was dying. By then I wasn't where I used to be, when she knew me. So she hired a private investigator to find me."

So she'd only contacted him when she'd had no other choice. Over a dozen years later. "Did you ever wonder?"

He shifted then, as if uncomfortable. She was a little—no, more than a little—surprised that he was answering her at all.

"Not much," he said, in the tone of an admission. "And not at all after a few weeks had passed. I figured she'd let me know if…"

"She knew where to find you, at first?"

"She could have reached me, yes."

"All right."

"Just like that? 'All right'?"

She shrugged. "If she could have reached you to tell you, it was obviously her choice."

She looked up as Malmsteen sounded again. Enough, she thought. Snow Patrol next week.

It was Craig Wilson, who waved and headed immediately for the bin of CDs.

"So about those rules," she said.

Jordy's father had glanced over as well, but when it was clear they weren't about to be intruded on, he turned back.

"So that's it? No recriminations for not con-
tacting her and asking?"

"Wow," she said. "Who chewed on you? I'm
assuming she was a responsible adult with
phone capabilities."

His mouth quirked yet again. "Guess I
haven't quite adjusted to the idea that I had
a kid all those years I never knew about. Not
that I know what I would have done if I had
known."

"The right thing."

He blinked, clearly startled. "How do you
know?"

She gestured toward the room where Jordy
was no doubt deep into practicing. "You're
doing it now. That tells me you probably would
have done it then."

He looked, in a word, dumbstruck. And she
wondered if no one had ever acknowledged
that that was what he was doing.

And then it hit her. How many people even
knew what the real circumstances were? That
he hadn't even known Jordy existed until the
boy's mother had no other choice? Marilyn,
who she had quickly learned was the root of the

very active Deer Creek grapevine, had simply referred to him as a widower with a son.

And she wondered if he wanted it that way, because it was easier, requiring no explanation.

Or maybe because it was easier on Jordy.

For the first time since she'd met the unhappy boy, she found herself willing to give his father at least that much credit.

"May I ask one more question?"

He gave her a sideways look that spoke volumes, pointing out without a word that she hadn't once asked for permission so far.

And yet, for the most part, he'd answered her, without much equivocation or even hesitation. She wondered if this might be the question that broke the string.

"When did you and Jordy's mom get married?"

He went very still. At the same time, that intensity she'd always felt from him heightened as he shifted to stare directly at her. Finally, just when she thought he wouldn't, he answered. And it was an answer that explained a great deal.

"Three hours before she died."

Chapter 8

When Mr. Wilson approached the counter, a CD in his hand, Wyatt was glad of the interruption. He backed up a step, indicating with a nod that the older man should go ahead.

He couldn't believe he'd told her that. But then, he couldn't believe a lot of what he'd told her. His desperation for help must run deeper than he'd realized. He didn't want to lose this fight, and a fight it was, for Jordy—Jordan, he corrected; he had to stop himself from using Jordy in his thoughts or he might slip up and use it aloud, and his son had made it quite clear he didn't like it. Except, apparently, from this woman.

"I've been thinking about ordering this," Mr. Wilson said, clearly pleased, "and here you had already gotten it in."

"Just for you," Kai said, smiling at the gray-haired man with the dapper goatee. "We share more tastes than just Segovia."

"Darlin'," Mr. Wilson said with an exaggerated drawl, "if I were thirty years younger, I'd be asking you to come listen with me."

"If you were ten years younger, I couldn't resist."

Craig Wilson laughed as she rang up the sale, and was whistling cheerfully as he walked out the door.

"Do all the men who come in flirt with you?" *Where the hell had that come from? He'd wanted a diversion from her last question, but—*

"Not all," she answered, her expression telling him she knew exactly what he'd done. "Some charge in like a raging bull," she added, her tone so pointed he winced inwardly. "But enough flirt to keep me smiling, so I'm not complaining."

"You ordered that CD especially for him?"

"I knew he'd want it as soon as they released it," she said. "I try to anticipate."

On the words the musical door chime—although the harsh metal guitar couldn't really be called a chime—sounded again. He had to give her points for cleverness on that; he had no idea what or who it was, but it had definitely caught his attention, just as it had the first time he'd come in here.

This time the customer was a teenager who looked about Jordan's age, eagerly picking up a CD Kai pulled from behind the counter. The girl, who gave him a sideways glance and a shy half smile, couldn't wait to hand over her carefully folded bills. She waved off the offered bag and clutched the case tightly as she ran out.

Wyatt lifted a brow.

"Soundtrack from the latest tween movie rage," Kai explained. "Clever marketing on their part, actually. You can download all the music, but they packaged the CD with exclusive stuff from the film, and a coupon for a free poster of the requisite heartthrob."

"You order that one ahead, too?"

"That one was a no-brainer," she said with a grin.

That grin came so easily, it seemed, and it lit up her face, made you want to at least smile back, even if you were feeling miserable. Which it seemed he was most of the time these days.

"I just hope I didn't miscalculate. There might be a few closet fans I don't know about."

Another customer, surprisingly Clark Bain, who ran the local gas station, arrived to pick up another item from behind the counter. The man nodded to him as Kai rang up something small and boxed. He focused on it, saw the image on the side of the box and realized it was a trumpet mouthpiece.

"Wyatt," Bain said.

"Clark," he returned.

"How's that SUV running?"

"Fine, since you replaced that fuel filter. Thanks."

"Good. I'm like Ms. Reynolds here, I like happy customers."

"Who plays the trumpet?" Wyatt asked after

the man had gone, knowing all of Clark's kids were grown by now.

"He does," she said, startling him.

"Clark Bain plays the trumpet?"

"Dixieland jazz, from what he told me. He wanted that particular mouthpiece."

Wyatt shook his head. Of all the things he might have guessed, that wasn't even on the list.

Another customer came and went, again with Kai handing over an order that had been re-served, guitar strings this time.

"Busy," he said when she was done this time.

"Special order Saturday," Kai said.

"You do a lot of special orders?

"It's my specialty."

He smiled in spite of himself at the wordplay. And somewhere in the back of his mind he was realizing this was the longest conversation he'd had with anyone in a very long time. And he was, much to his shock, enjoying it.

"I've promoted that from the beginning," she said. "There are advantages to being a bit remote, it makes people weigh the cost and time and hassle of a forty-mile trip to the near-

est mall or big box store against the conve-
nience of being able to pick their items up here,
usually only a day or two later."

She was, he realized, not just smart and perceptive, she was practical. And apparently had
the good business sense to realize she couldn't
beat the huge competitors on their field, so she
played on another one, personalized service.
So far it had worked, and word of mouth had
helped, even drawing people from well outside
Deer Creek.

"Especially when you know what they'll
want in advance?"

She shrugged. "It's all a matter of paying attention, learning people's tastes. And then extrapolation."

"Extrapolation?"

"You know, 'If you like this, you might also
like that,'" she said.

He studied her for a moment. "That takes a
lot of knowledge."

"A bit. And I didn't know much about
some things a few people in town like. I expected country, but I had no idea there was
such a call for classical. Fell victim to my own

stereotypes." She admitted it so easily it charmed him.

"It's tough for most people to face that they have a bias, let alone to change it."

"But we should."

"Unless it's a validly founded one," he said. "I have a severe prejudice against black widow spiders."

"Ew. Me, too. I avoid them scrupulously."

"Wise. Unless one gets in your house. Then you go after it."

She shivered, and he wasn't sure if it was feigned or real. "Or stay up all night obsessing about where it's hiding."

"I prefer a proactive approach," he said. And there it was, he thought. The crux of the whole problem with his son; he'd forgotten one of the basic tenets. "Which is something I forgot about with Jordan. I just kept reacting to what he did."

"Or didn't do?"

He nodded. Made himself go on, feeling he owed her this. "You were right. I was focused so much on the bad things I was trying to keep him out of, I didn't even think about what good things I could be getting him into."

"I… Thank you," she said, as if his words had been the last thing she'd ever expected.

"I can be reasonable, contrary to what my son has probably told you." He sighed. "Contrary to what just about anybody has probably told you. Haven't shown much reason since Jordan and I got back here."

"It's hard to be reasonable when you're scared," she said.

"Scared?" That wasn't a word he'd often heard applied to himself.

"Of losing him, to those bad things."

Something dark and bleak shadowed her eyes for a moment. He remembered what he'd read.

"You know about that, don't you."

It wasn't a question, since he already knew the answer.

"Do some checking up, did you?"

He didn't bother to deny it. "Yes." And then, feeling he owed her this as well, he added, "Something I should have done before I… charged in here the first time."

"That would have been nice, yes," she agreed.

And then, with a rather decisive nod, she finished her computer entry, apparently on the change in her string inventory, and looked at him.

"About that. There is somebody I wanted to tell you about."

He lifted a brow, staying silent this time.

"He's an older boy, maybe twenty-two or twenty-three, I'm not positive. But he's been… friendly to Jordy."

Wyatt tensed. "Friendly?"

"Not in a nasty way," she said hastily. "Just odd. Since he's so much older. And Jordy sort of…revels in it. He likes that an older boy, one he thinks is the height of cool, pays attention to him."

Wyatt frowned. "Who is this boy?"

"His name is Max Middleton. He's got a bit of a rough reputation, although he's never done anything I can put my finger on. It's just that it seems odd that he's so friendly to a thirteen-year-old when most guys his age couldn't be bothered. Like his two buddies he hangs with all the time, they act like you'd expect, impatient with him and annoyed that this little kid pesters them."

Wyatt filed the name away to be checked on later. "Thank you," he said, finally, a little wary of saying anything else, now that she'd finally told him this. It seemed to work, because she went on.

"I don't know what his story is, so maybe there's a reason, maybe he lost a little brother or something, but…" She shrugged. "I thought you should know."

He didn't react to her too-nice speculation— women tended to do that, he thought, look for some way to understand rather than simply dealing with the action—just marveled a bit at the change from the woman who had challenged him at every turn the first time he'd… well, charged in here. And definitely a change from the woman who'd subtly warned him about minding his own business, he thought. Apparently she'd realized Jordan was his business. Right now his only business. Of course, now that they'd talked, civilly, for a while, she—

"I'm not late!"

Jordan's exclamation came from the back of the store, and they both turned as the boy closed the door to the sound room and came toward them.

"It's one hour, exactly, so you can't be mad."

Startled, Wyatt lifted his wrist to check his watch. He really should get something simpler, he thought; the multifunction chronograph was overkill for his life now. But it was also accurate to within the tiniest split of a second, and what it told him was that he'd been standing here talking for Jordan's full hour. He wasn't sure what shocked him more, that he'd done it, or that it had gone by so quickly.

Jordan was looking at him warily, as if he expected him to erupt, even though he was right, it was one hour on the mark.

"Then let's go," he said evenly, suddenly as eager to leave as Jordan was reluctant.

The boy was silent once they were back in the truck. He'd driven because they were going to the auto parts store on the far edge of town, with an oil change and tire rotation on the schedule for tomorrow. He could take it to Clark and have him do it, probably a lot more quickly and efficiently, but he collected these tasks to fill up his weekends the way his mother had collected recipes, certain there could never be too many. And he refused to admit it was to make sure he didn't have too much time to think. About anything.

And now he had one more thing to add to that not-thinking-about-it list—Kai Reynolds. And the fact that the hour spent with her had been the swiftest, and the most pleasant he'd passed in longer than he could remember.

He told himself she was merely a puzzle. An interesting dichotomy, the savvy business-woman and the flashy girl in the photograph.

"Have you ever heard her play? Other than recordings, I mean?"

He hadn't meant to ask, but he'd been saying a lot of things he hadn't meant to lately.

Jordan gave him a sideways look, Wyatt guessed weighing his reluctance to talk to him at all against his eagerness to talk about all things Kai. He stayed silent, letting the calculations go on, until the eagerness won.

"Yeah. It was amazing."

"She's good?"

"Better than good."

The boy hesitated, and again Wyatt stayed silent. It was the least contentious conversation they'd had in a while, and he didn't want to disrupt it.

"Once I thought the guitar was out of tune. She took it, checked it, then played this really wicked riff."

Jordan rubbed at his fingertips. Sore, no doubt, Wyatt thought, wondering if there was anything that would help toughen them up.

"She said the main difference between what came out of it when she played and when I did was hours and hours of practice."

"And tougher fingers." Wyatt thought he saw, for the briefest moment, the boy's mouth move toward a smile.

"Yeah," Jordan admitted.

He continued to rub at his fingers. Silently. But it was a whole different kind of silence than their usual strained hush. And after a couple of minutes, Jordan said, as if it meant nothing to him, "There are some videos up on YouTube. Of her band. She really rocked."

"I'll bet," Wyatt said, wondering if that

had been a suggestion to check them out. He wouldn't, of course. Kai Reynolds was already taking up too many brain cells, and he needed them all just to deal with his son.

He wondered if he should ask about this Max. His instincts were telling him to push, while the boy was actually speaking to him.

He didn't.

And when he realized that he didn't follow those instincts because he didn't want to lose even this tiny bit of peace they'd reached, however transitory it might be, he knew he was losing it.

It's a tough gig....

Kai's sympathetic words echoed in his head. And renewed his determination. Single parents all over the country handled it, managed, dealt. He would too, somehow.

His inward pep talk helped, for about as long as it took them to pick up the supplies for the oil change and get home. When Jordan realized he was expected to help with the chore tomorrow, his protest was instant.

"But my hands hurt!"

"Your choice. That you've taken up playing doesn't change the work that needs to be done here."

And just like that the brief, tentative cease-fire was over as Jordan mouthed a curse he wasn't quite angry enough to say out loud.

"That's twice I've ignored that word," Wyatt said. "You don't get a third pass."

Jordan flushed. And lapsed into the sullen silence that seemed his predominant mood.

Nice work, Blake, Wyatt muttered to himself.

Tough gig indeed.

Chapter 9

Kai drew in a deep, happy breath; nothing soothed like the smell of fresh baked bread, especially on a rainy fall day. She was going to learn how to fill her own place with that luscious scent someday, but for now the little bakery filled her carb needs perfectly. She'd stopped for some of their wonderful garlic bread to go with her spaghetti tonight, and had been unable to resist a loaf of their signature sweet apple spice bread for breakfast.

She dutifully asked about Mrs. Day's daughter, who was away at college, and smiled attentively at the proud mother's response. As she took the proffered bag, she thanked the woman and waved a cheerful goodbye.

Despite the rain, the usual group was at Dinozzo's Pizza, sheltered under the striped awning, and she'd had to park a block down. She could have walked instead of driven, she thought wryly, and gotten just about as wet.

She unlocked the door of her little coupe and set the bread inside, then straightened to get in. Something caught her eye over in front of Dinozzo's, and for a moment she focused on the group of four at the corner of the building. Max, she saw, and his two buddies, and another guy, a kid really, maybe sixteen. Max made a gesture, and then he and the younger boy disappeared around the building into the alley. That was the second time she'd seen that series of actions, she thought.

The rain was picking up, and she dived for the shelter of the car. Moments later she was pulling into her small garage in the back of the store. When she'd remodeled the building, she'd had them add that even though it took up some floor space; customer parking was more important. Plus, in the garage was a stairway that led to her apartment, which made days like this easier. And drier.

She managed to fight off her other thoughts until she had finished her meal. She ate inside tonight, with some plaintive Celtic music that seemed to fit her mood playing softly. Then the scenario from the pizza parlor ran back in her head like the replay of a video.

And she had to finally admit the nature of what she had seen. The small cluster of people, the quick gesture and the disappearance into a darkened alley despite the rain, and the fact that both Max and the younger boy had been reaching into their pockets as they vanished into the shadows. And most damning, the furtiveness of it all, the glance over the shoulder to see if anyone who could cause trouble was watching, and the watchful stance of Daniel and Brian, the third of the trio.

An image flashed through her mind, not for the first time, of Max's wad of cash, mostly small bills. Favors?

Party favors, maybe.

It was all painfully familiar.

She hated the idea that Jordy's father might have been right. That he might truly have reason to be concerned. Reason to be as suspicious as he was. She hated all of it.

But she hated what might be going on more. And she couldn't deny it or ignore it just because Jordy's father rubbed her the wrong way and she didn't want to agree with him. Because denial had only one consequence.

The memory of Kit and his addiction to lethal chemicals was hovering. The media had always phrased it in terms of him losing his battle with drugs. She knew better. Kit had never really battled them at all, in fact he embraced them, savoring the easier availability the further up the success ladder they went.

He'd teased Kai about her aversion to the stuff, calling her straightlaced and worse. At first it had been a gentle, sort of wistful teasing, as if he admired her steadfastness. But, as everything else, it had gotten worse as his addiction deepened, until it was no longer teasing but a driven, malevolent sniping, as if he were determined to drag her down with him.

She stood and gathered her dishes with sharp, angry movements. She didn't want to deal with this. She'd had enough of it. All she wanted to do was focus on her business, and getting her online presence going to supplement the brick and mortar side. She'd meant to have that done long ago, but so far all she'd managed was to have a small but steady flow of orders for her own favorite guitar strings coming in. She needed to make a final choice on suppliers for the rest of the products she envisioned, and at the same time needed a revamp of her now fairly minimalistic website, and she had the time to do neither.

So quit eating, she told herself. *Save the prep, eating and cleanup time.*

She almost smiled at the realization that she would do that before she would cut into her playing time, those times after the store was closed when she would pick whatever guitar she had that struck her fancy and disappear into the back room herself for an hour or two's indulgence.

But the reality of what she'd seen tonight quickly made the smile fade.

She sighed as she slammed the dishwasher shut and dried her hands on the towel that was one of the set her mother had bought for her after she'd visited and seen the results of the remodel. She'd pronounced the final results a great improvement, but Kai knew she was biting back a comment about how it would be even better somewhere in civilization. Her mother was a city girl to the bone, and she often seemed bemused that her daughter had such a preference for something so foreign to her own soul.

Again the attempt at distraction failed after a few moments. And she finally resigned herself. She would have to talk to Jordy's father. It wouldn't be so bad, she told herself. He'd been quite civil this afternoon, and he had changed his mind about letting Jordy play. So obviously he was capable of being, as he'd said, reasonable.

So she would tell him. But that would be the end of her involvement. Let him handle it. She didn't want to be the bad guy, warning Jordy off the "friend" he was in a little awe of.

Besides, she thought wryly, Jordy already hated his dad, how much worse could it get?

Even as she thought it she felt a nudge of guilt; the guy seemed to care, seemed to be really trying, even if he did come off like an overbearing bully sometimes.

So she would talk to him. She had to. For Jordy's sake. And if Jordy felt betrayed, she'd just have to deal with it.

She went to bed early, the memories hovering, knowing that tonight would be one of those nights when in sleep she would lose the battle to keep them at bay.

Yes, Jordy might feel she'd betrayed him by talking to his father.

But at least he'd be alive to feel that way.

Wyatt sat staring at the screen. He'd done his usual check of Jordan's personal page. Tonight was the get-together some of his "friends" were pushing him to go to, so he knew he needed to be extra watchful. He had studied the photo of the most vocal of the urgers, a guy who looked to be in his early twenties and went by the initials MM. He wondered, if he printed out that picture and showed it to Kai Reynolds, if she would recognize him. If perhaps this was the very person she'd been talking about.

And that thought had led him to Jordan's

earlier words. Which had led him to YouTube. And the videos that had him mesmerized.

She had, indeed, as Jordan had said, rocked. Most of them were from what had turned out to be the band's final tour, about five and a half years ago. They were mostly amateur jobs, with tiny, low-resolution cameras on cell phones, or larger ones apparently smuggled into the venue by members of the obviously enthusiastic crowd. And crowd there was; when that blogger had referred to them as having the potential to be the next big thing, he hadn't been exaggerating.

There were a couple of clips that had been done by the venue itself, higher quality and much better sound. So while the others showed the enthusiasm of the crowd, it was these he watched most closely. And repeatedly.

This was the woman in that photograph. Same guitar. Same wild mane of red hair that flew with her movements. Different outfit, this time a blue, metallic, snug-fitting top that almost matched her guitar, and showed a bit more than a hint of feminine curves. White, skintight jeans that did the same. And an expression on her face that indicated she was only peripherally aware of that packed house of fans, and totally aware of the amazing sounds that were flowing from beneath her fingers.

Because they were amazing. He was no expert, but the talent there was obvious, in the way she went from loud, powerful solos and jamming windups on upbeat numbers to a whisper delicate accompaniment to a slow, sweet ballad. She sang on that one, on the chorus, and her low husky voice made his stomach knot in a strange way. Hudson might have had more powerful pipes, but Kai's voice and the way she wrapped it around the plaintive lyrics could make you weep.

He made himself look at the front man. Kai certainly kept her eyes on him. And he fancied it was more than with the eyes of a lover, although that was certainly there in the way she tracked him. And oddly, although this was dated almost six years ago, she looked younger now. At the least, less troubled. But maybe he was only imagining the worry, the pain, and as he watched the last video in the series again, the despair.

But he didn't think he was.

She knew.

With all the certainty of an onlooker helpless to stop an oncoming disaster, she knew what was coming.

It took him a moment after he shut down the browser and pulled the earphones off for him to realize what that strange tightness in his chest was. He was aching for her, and her loss. She'd been in love with an addict and the end was inevitable, but he was hurting for her anyway, something he didn't quite understand.

And he realized this was the first time he'd felt much of anything for anyone outside of his own suddenly overturned life.

Don't give fate any levers to use against you.

He wasn't sure where the old advice had originated, but he couldn't argue with its validity, especially now. Because Jordan was definitely a lever, and keeping him safe had trumped all else since the moment he'd read that warning email.

A sudden memory struck him, of a reputed crime boss who'd been taken into custody in a dramatic gunfight. It had been all over the news, caught by security cameras. In the battle the man's son had been killed, and the hardened criminal's agonized response had captured the morbid fascination of the entire country. At the time, and given the fact that the dead son had been a crazed sociopath responsible for more deaths than would probably ever be discovered, Wyatt had thought Phillip Stark's reaction a bit false and overwrought.

Now he wasn't so sure.

Old friends would laugh at him now, he thought, laugh at the idea of him being in the most permanent, unbreakable relationship there was, that of parent. Girlfriends, wives, might come and go, but nothing could ever change the fact that Jordan was his son.

Or that being a father was the hardest thing he'd ever tried to do, and given his past, that was saying something. He thrived on difficult challenges everywhere else, but on the personal side, he was miserable at it. The best thing he could do was avoid adding to the lousy track record he'd already compiled.

Besides, it wasn't like he had the time or energy for anything else now, not with Jordan.

Especially the kind of time and energy somebody like Kai Reynolds would require.

Uh-oh.

The internal warning sounded loud and clear. It had been a while since he'd heard it, simply because for the last year he'd been focused on leaving the past behind, and for the last six months it had taken all he had to get used to the idea he was a father.

That's what he got for wasting time pondering stupid things. Thinking that way about any woman was idiocy at the moment. Thinking about this one was absurd. He'd have been better off with someone like Jordan's mother, who, even as the end neared, worried about keeping her promises.

Melissa's image came back to him. "You know I never meant this to happen this way," she'd said yet again as she lay dying. "I never blamed you. I promised you no recriminations, no fallout, and I meant it. I never wanted you to even know. That's why I gave him my last name."

"I know," he'd said. It was impossible not to when he was reeling from the discovery that she'd kept secret the biggest fallout of their single time together.

"That's why I never told you about him. I didn't want him to come looking for you, when he…grew up."

She'd broken down then, at the reminder that she wouldn't see that happen. Sometimes that particular, vivid, painful memory was the only thing that kept him going, prevented him from throwing up his hands and walking away after a tough day of dealing with the boy who now slept upstairs.

Or was supposed to be sleeping, he thought suddenly, realizing he'd been held so rapt by those videos that he'd forgotten the reason for watching Jordan closely tonight.

He shut down the computer, and when the screen went dark so did the room, except for the angled shafts of silver light coming through the windows from the gibbous moon that had broken through the scattering rain clouds. He'd grown up in this house, and needed no extra lighting to find his way around. He sat there, in the dark silence, telling himself to get up and check on his son. But the images he'd just seen and the music he'd just heard kept playing back in his head.

He glanced at his watch. The numbers glowed clearly; it was ten minutes before the prescribed meet-up time. On the thought, he heard a sound from upstairs. With a sigh, he got up and went to the back of the house, still without turning a light on. He unlocked and slipped out the back door silently. He moved with an easy stealth toward the big oak tree. He stood in its dark shadow, waiting.

He held his breath as he watched Jordan stretch to make it from his bedroom window to the still-wet tree branch. He moved a little closer; it wouldn't be the first time he'd had to catch a falling child. He was angry with himself that it was even a possibility. If he hadn't been so lost in idiotic meanderings, he would have been upstairs in time to stop him from getting this far. But by the time he'd heard the window slide open, it was too late, and besides, his instinct was to cut off, not chase.

Jordan made it, and worked his way down the big tree.

"Going somewhere?"

Jordan gasped as he dropped the last three feet and he stumbled and sprawled literally at his father's feet. The boy stared up at him, his eyes wide. Even with only the moonlight, Wyatt could see his expression was a mix of anger and confusion and resignation.

"Yeah, you're busted," he said.

Jordan said nothing as he slowly got to his feet. For an instant something else flickered across his face, and Wyatt knew he was thinking about running.

"You know I'll catch you," he said quietly, startling Jordan further. "The only difference is I'll be madder."

They'd been through a chase once before, and Wyatt had been glad he'd kept in shape; running the three miles to work and back three or four times a week had been worth it. He was going to have to do something else now, though, because he didn't dare be unable to respond quickly for the twenty minutes or so the run took.

He saw the moment when Jordan gave up. The boy's shoulders sagged and his head lowered as he trudged back into the house. Back in his room, Wyatt picked up the discarded pajamas from the floor and tossed them at the boy.

"In case you're thinking about trying again, I'll be up."

Jordan muttered something as he got ready for bed the second time tonight.

"You're lucky. If I was really mad, you'd be sleeping downstairs, literally under my nose."

"Yeah, like you're not really mad," Jordan said, disbelief clear in his tone.

Wyatt shrugged. "Annoyed, but not furious. You have to test the limits, I guess."

Jordan looked startled.

"And this," Wyatt added, "is an immovable one."

It wasn't until Jordan was back in bed that he spoke again. "How did you know?"

Wyatt wasn't about to divulge his source, Jordan's own social page, so he purposely answered as if the boy had meant something else.

"Because that tree's how I would have gotten out, if it was me."

"Yeah, right," Jordan muttered.

Wyatt walked to the door. Then turned back.

"It's how I *did* sneak out, when I was a kid. That's how I knew."

Jordan, who had just laid down, sat back up. "This was your room?"

"Yes." He gestured at the doorknob. "That's why it locks from the outside. And why there's a keyed lock on that window."

"You used to sneak out that window?"

Wyatt leaned against the doorjamb. "A couple of times. And I regretted it. It's a lot harder to sneak in than out. My father always knew."

Jordan eyed him warily. "What did he do?"

"He put that lock on it. And made my life a living hell for the next month," Wyatt said.

The boy grimaced. "Mine couldn't get much worse."

"Oh, trust me, it could," Wyatt said, remembering the days of exhaustion as his father gave him long lists of chores that had to be finished after school, along with his homework, and if they weren't done when the old man got home he had to stay up until they were, no matter how long it took. After a couple of days of just a few hours of sleep, he was too tired to even think about anything else. Which was, of course, the plan.

Jordan was looking at him with anger, distrust, suspicion. Wyatt sighed inwardly. He didn't want this. He felt like he was floundering helplessly, in way over his head.

"You get a pass this once," he told his son. "But don't try it again. And this door stays open."

"You gonna stay up all night and watch me?" A trace of a sneer had slipped into the boy's voice, and Wyatt pushed away from the doorjamb and told himself not to react to the tone.

"If necessary. Wouldn't be the first time."

He felt Jordan's gaze on him as he flipped out the light and headed down the hall.

It was going to be a long night.

Chapter 10

Kai locked up the front door of Play On and stuffed the keys into her pocket. No rain today, it had stopped last evening and this morning had been brisk and smelled wonderful in the way only a rain-washed world can.

She'd had a fairly busy day, with the first delivery of band instruments arriving, and kids and parents trickling in all day to pick them up, some happy about it, some resentful, clearly being forced into it. Many of those talked to her about how they'd much rather play a guitar than a clarinet.

She always leaned in then and whispered to the reluctant child, "If you show your folks you're willing to work at this, I bet they'll let you do the guitar later."

The older kids tended to roll their eyes but smile, the younger ones took her words to heart, and the parents were happy with her. She supposed they'd expected her to side with the guitar-leaning kids, given her own history.

But the one who didn't show up today was Jordy. He always turned up on Mondays, anxious to catch up after the weekend away. She hoped he wasn't sick.

Or that his father hadn't changed his mind.

She started to walk toward the bank, dodging some of the puddles that remained after yesterday's rain. The day's business had netted more than she was comfortable leaving around, so she was going to make an extra deposit tonight, and probably would need to for the next couple of days as the instruments went out the door.

She was musing about how nice it was to be able to walk down the street with a sizeable amount of cash and checks without worrying. And smiling at the additional credit and debit card receipts already in the system. Play On would make it through the winter again. Funny how that gave her nearly as much satisfaction as a sellout crowd had once given her on the road.

She was about to pull open the bank door when it was opened in front of her, by a man with a troubled expression. He saw her, his expression changed to a smile, and he held the door for her. John Hunt, she realized, owner of the packaging plant. She didn't know him that well, knew his wife and daughter better, but he was unfailingly courteous and friendly when they did run into each other. She liked him. And he reminded her somewhat of her father, so she spoke to him with respect.

"Thank you, Mr. Hunt," she said as she stepped inside.

The man nodded. "Hello, Kai. Did Catherine make it in to pick up the detested violin?"

She was startled, then laughed. "Yes, yes she did."

He let the door close for the moment. "It was my wife's idea. Catherine thinks it's the most boring instrument ever made."

"I used to feel the same way." Kai looked thoughtful. "Send her in sometime. I'll play her some Celtic fiddle music, might change her mind. It pretty much rocks."

The man's brows lifted. "That might help. She's got visions of nothing but classical music in her future."

"Always a good place to start, but it doesn't mean you have to stay there."

The smile widened. "Thank you," he said. "I'll tell her. When I get a free second," he added in a rueful tone.

"Problems?" Kai remembered his troubled expression.

"Just some strange goings-on out at the plant. A prowler. Or prowlers."

That was odd enough in quiet Deer Creek to merit surprise. "Wow. Any idea who?"

He shook his head.

"You have security out there, don't you?"

"We do. But not as much as we may need, if this keeps up. I'm working on that."

Another bank customer came in, putting a pause on the conversation. Which gave her a moment to make what was probably a foolish decision. Because she had just remembered John Hunt was Wyatt Blake's boss. And he had a reputation of being very aware of his employees' situations and needs. So if the boy was sick—or not—he might know.

"Do you know if Jordan Price is all right?"

The man frowned. "Wyatt Blake's boy?"

"I'm just wondering, because he usually comes into the store afternoons, to practice. But he didn't today. And…there was some tension between he and his father recently."

Mr. Hunt grimaced. "That's true on any given day," he said. "Wyatt's taken on a tough job. But I suppose it's nothing compared to what he's used to."

"What he's used to?"

Mr. Hunt gave her a startled, then guarded look. "Sorry. I shouldn't be talking about him when you asked about his boy. I think he's all right."

She wondered if there was more to the man's quick change than just a desire to answer the question she'd actually asked.

"Wyatt's in today, as usual," he said. "Or was. He gets off at three, when Jordan gets out of school."

Kai lifted a brow, surprised. "He does?"

The man nodded. "It's part of our agreement. Any additional work that needs doing, he does from home." He nodded his head in approval. "He's doing everything right, for that boy."

...he wouldn't even have that job if old man Hunt didn't owe him a favor.

Jordy's words came back to her, and she wondered what kind of favor Wyatt Blake had done for this man.

"It was good of you to give him that job, so that he could bring Jordy here like he wanted to."

Mr. Hunt grimaced again. "I owe him that and much more. I would have given him any job he wanted. Still can't believe he insisted on that one."

The man shook his head sharply, and before Kai could formulate another question he politely took his leave and was gone. Making her wonder if he'd again said something he thought he shouldn't have.

I owe him that much and more....

So Jordy had been right. And just how had that come about? What favor had Wyatt Blake done for John Hunt?

And why, why, *why* was she spending so much time worrying about it? No man had sapped as much of her thoughts and attention in years. That it was Jordan's too severe father was beyond irritating. Yet there he was, constantly niggling at the edge of her mind.

When Tuesday came and went, still with no Jordy, her concern spiked into worry. She hoped they hadn't fought again. Jordan had been so excited about playing that he'd quickly gotten over his dilemma about actually obeying his father. Perhaps he'd gone somewhere? Had his father sent him off to some relative she didn't know about?

Although Jordy hadn't mentioned any plans, and from his frequent grumblings she knew travel anywhere beyond the nearest sizable town, forty miles distant, for necessities that couldn't be found in Deer Creek, just didn't happen. They never went anywhere, just stuck here in boredom town, he often complained. And he, like her mother, couldn't wrap his mind around the idea that she herself loved it here.

"How could you? I mean, you used to tour,

go all these cool places, how can you stand to just stay here in boring Deer Creek?"

"Maybe because I did do all that traveling," she said. *And because a lot of the memories attached to those times aren't pleasant ones,* she'd added to herself.

By the end of Wednesday, she knew she had to do something. So when she closed up at five, instead of heading upstairs, she locked up and went for a walk. She had an excuse, she thought, it had been raining hard for two days straight, and it was nice to be able to walk without getting soaked.

At least, that's what she told herself as she headed for the big, Craftsman-style house. She was going for a walk anyway, it might as well be that way, so she could find out if Jordy was all right. It was just a neighborly thing to do, she told herself, checking on him.

She even believed it.

Almost.

Chapter 11

Wyatt heard the thump from upstairs, and guessed Jordan had thrown something yet again. Between that and the frequent slamming of the bathroom door— *If he really needed the bathroom that often, I'd have him off to the doctor,* Wyatt had thought wryly after the fourth time the slam had echoed through the house—he was making his feelings known.

Wyatt turned back to the laptop. The final data sheet he'd uploaded to his workstation at HP finished, and he was done for the day. It had taken a little longer than usual, because he'd had Jordan to deal with, but it was done. It had to be; he didn't want John to regret allowing him to work this way.

He stretched, thinking he might have to get a more substantial chair for this setup, because after a solid hour and a half hunched over the laptop keyboard he was feeling it.

Or you're just flat-out getting old, he told himself.

He felt old. He'd felt that way for a long time now. And dealing with Jordan only emphasized it. Some parts of this made the old days look simple. Not that he wanted to go back, but at least things had been more clear-cut, the path more obvious. He—

The alert popped up.

He toyed with the idea of avoiding it for a while. But ignoring it wasn't going to make it go away. Besides, there might be crucial info in it.

Maybe he found an innocent explanation for it all, Wyatt thought, then laughed aloud at the absurdity of that. In that world, there were no innocent explanations. Not many, anyway. And that knowledge was so deeply ingrained he doubted he'd ever get past it.

He worked his way through the same intricate steps, until finally he had the message open in front of him.

Checked around. I wasn't the only one. Others about the same time contacted by different people looking for you. All should be friendlies, but double heads up.

The message ended with an offer of help if he needed it. Did he? He didn't know. He'd gotten rusty, he knew that, but so bad that he couldn't handle this?

If it had been just him, he wouldn't have even blinked. But it wasn't just him anymore.

...friendlies.

Not friends, friendlies. A fine but definite line. Because he wasn't crowded with old friends. The one who had sent these messages was one of a very few. And also one of the even fewer who knew where he was. The question was, had one of the others who knew also been contacted? Had his location already been compromised? Did he need to—

A knock on the door startled him. He told himself an enemy wasn't likely to come politely knocking on his door, stifling a scornful laugh at himself. He deleted the message and quickly keyed in the shutdown command, waited for the familiar desktop screen to reappear, a process that took about ninety seconds. He was half wishing whoever it was would just go away, but by the time he was at the desktop the knock came again.

He knew who it was long before he got the door open. The mission-style front door had a bank of windows across the top, and he caught the gleam of afternoon sunlight on rich, red hair.

Kai.

He stopped in his tracks, a foot away from the door. He stared at the doorknob as if it held the answer, but he wasn't sure there *was* an answer to this, this crazy surge of heat and tangled feelings that threatened to swamp him every time he thought of her.

Which was too damned often, he told himself.

It was crazy. Completely insane. He'd checked her out, because of Jordan. He needed to know who his son was spending time around. But it should have ended there. Once he'd determined she wasn't—or at least didn't seem to be—a threat, it should have ended there. She shouldn't have been popping into his head at any odd moment, shouldn't have had him thinking about what excuse he could come up with to stop into Play On, shouldn't have had him going back to watch those videos time and again.

And she sure as hell shouldn't have been populating his dreams. Vivid, sharp and uncomfortably hot dreams. He'd thought anything would be an improvement on the nightmares he'd battled for so long, but this new development only made things worse. Because somehow the two would get tangled up together, and he was dreaming of loss before he even had it to lose.

And you're not going to get it, he told himself. *You're not even going to try. That's the last thing you need to throw into this mix.*

Self-lecture complete, he reached to open the door.

She was at the bottom of the steps, as if she'd given up and was leaving. If he'd hung on a few more seconds, he might have escaped this after all. He wondered why the idea didn't please him more.

At the sound of the door she turned back. Looked at him. Smiled. Took his breath away, literally. And for a moment he forgot how to get it back.

"Kai," he said, an instant later wishing he'd stuck with a more formal "Ms. Reynolds."

"Wyatt," she said as she came back up the steps onto the covered porch, and he changed his mind; not for anything would he have traded the sound of his name in her voice, even in a casual greeting that meant little.

"What are you—"

He stopped, surprised at the odd sound of his own voice, at the tightness, the strain in it.

"—doing here?" she finished for him, as if she hadn't noticed. "I was out for a walk, and I thought I'd come by and make sure Jordy's okay. He hasn't been in, and I was afraid maybe you changed your mind about letting him play."

He stepped outside and pulled the door shut behind him; this was not a conversation he wanted his son to overhear. He supposed he should be thankful she was concerned enough about his son to come checking. But he wasn't at all sure that was what he was feeling.

"Only temporarily," he said.

To her credit, she merely waited, one arched brow raised in inquiry.

"He's…grounded at the moment."

She drew back slightly. "Using the music as a weapon?" she asked.

"It's the only one that seems to get through to him," he admitted.

"Not worried that using it against him will guarantee he'll never trust you with anything else you can use against him?"

He stared at her. She couldn't know, there was no way, but he couldn't seem to stop Jordan's furious words from echoing in his head.

I wish you'd never found out. Next time I'll make sure you never do.

"Oh, he trusts me," he said, not even caring if he sounded bitter. "To ruin his life."

To his surprise, she smiled. "That's in a parent's job description, I think. So, what did he do?"

"Sneaked out his window to meet up with

some people he knows from online. One of them was the booze supplier."

He didn't know how he expected her to react. He didn't even know why he was telling her at all, except that she did have sort of a sideways interest in the matter.

"Ouch. Not good."

That surprised him. It must have shown in his face, because she went on.

"To this day I get emails from strangers who have…certain ideas about me because of an image they've culled mostly from online information. I know about the power, and potential for fakery that's inherent there."

He stared at her, more than a little startled at the concise, articulate summation.

"So, how long does it cost him to have disobeyed an order?"

His mouth quirked. "I never gave him an order. He never even asked to go."

"Just sneaked out?"

"I presume he knew I'd say no, so didn't bother with the formalities."

She studied him for a moment. "What was

the last thing you said 'yes' to? Besides letting him play, I mean, since that was an order?"

There wasn't a hint of criticism in her tone, but he winced inwardly anyway.

"I...don't remember. He doesn't ask much. He seems to just do it, then waits to get in trouble."

Again there was a long pause as she looked at him. He wondered what she was thinking, was suddenly anxious to know what was going on behind those smoky gray eyes.

"Anything about that seem familiar?" she asked, her tone just a bit too casual now.

"Your point?" he asked.

"Just that all kids do it to some extent. Easier to beg forgiveness than ask permission and all that. I did it. And I'm willing to bet you did, too."

He let out a compressed breath. "I was the expert on it," he said. "But the situation was different."

"Because of your father."

Why on earth had he ever told her so much? He didn't talk about his father to anybody.

A little desperate to change the subject, he grasped at something uppermost in his mind.

"I watched some video Jordan told me about. Of Relative Fusion."

The complete non sequitur made her blink. He waited for her to ask what he thought; all performers wanted to know that, didn't they?

Instead, after a moment she just said, "Well, if he's talking to you that much, maybe there's hope after all."

Focus, he thought. She was focused on Jordan, that's why she was here, and she wasn't going to be distracted. A good attribute, in most cases. He wouldn't be alive today if he wasn't good at staying focused. But right now, he wished she had a little less of the ability.

"It's about the only thing he's spoken to me about. So I watched."

Again he paused, but the expected question didn't come.

"There are a bunch out there," she said neutrally. "We were never manic about stopping cameras, or recorders for that matter."

"Why?"

She shrugged. "We figured it was our job to

be good enough that they'd want the quality of a professional recording. Or songs we didn't do live."

He hesitated, then said quietly, "You were good."

She nodded. "We were."

He liked that she didn't dissemble, didn't even thank him. He wondered if the barely perceptible tension that was showing around her mouth and eyes was for the loss of the music, or the man she'd loved.

"You miss it?"

"I miss the music, sometimes. The rest? Not really. Oh, it was exhilarating, good for the ego, but the spotlight had some pretty hefty downsides."

"You didn't claim the spotlight often," he said. *Not nearly as often as you should have,* he added to himself.

She shrugged. "Didn't want it. There's still a bias in the world, about girls with guitars. It took me a while to realize it."

"Even good-looking girls with guitars?"

"Especially," she said. "At first I played it up, until I realized people were assuming that was why I was there, for looks, not because I was a damned good guitarist."

A realization struck him, based on something he'd noticed in the progression of videos he'd watched.

"You changed the lighting," he said. "On your solos."

He had the great pleasure of seeing surprise fill her expressive face. She was looking at him as if he'd done something totally unexpected. Which told him a lot about what she expected. From him, anyway.

But he knew he was right. He'd noticed the change right away, probably because he was so focused on her as he watched, not the band as a whole, or even the admittedly charismatic and talented front man.

"I wanted them listening, not looking," she said simply.

And she'd accomplished it with one simple change, he thought. The lighting had gone from a standard spotlight on her during her extensive and blazing solo riffs, to a narrow, focused spot on just her hands and the guitar. On what was, to her, most important. Not her appearance, or the response those flashy, wild looks got her.

"You left the spotlight to Hudson."

He watched her for any sign of pained reaction to the mention of the name. He saw only a flash of sadness.

"He was the one they should be watching, anyway."

"You loved him."

"I did. But in the end, I didn't respect him very much."

"I read he tried, went into rehab."

She lifted a brow at him. "You have been doing homework."

"You're important to my son." He wished that was all it was. Wished it was that simple. Wished he wasn't pretty sure his interest went far beyond Jordan.

"In a way, that brings me to something I wanted to tell you."

He'd been so caught up in the simple fact that she was talking to him that he drew back slightly, wary of whatever was coming.

"That guy I told you about? The older boy who's so friendly with Jordy?"

He nodded, the wariness growing.

"I'm afraid he…may be into something nastier than I thought."

Wyatt listened as she told him what she'd seen, and what it had made her suspect. He knew he was more suspicious than most, it was part of who he was, long ingrained now. But he sometimes couldn't believe how naive others could be. And right now, he couldn't believe that someone who'd lived in the world she'd lived in for a while could have had any doubts about what was going on, what Max Middleton was up to.

The only question was what it had to do with Jordan. The worry that had been building throughout her explanation peaked as she finished.

"I have no proof, really—"

"It's only obvious," he snapped. "Why the hell didn't you tell me this before?"

Others, people with supposedly a lot more nerve than the average person, had backed off when his temper bit. Kai Reynolds held her ground.

"Because I had even less proof before."

"You wanted him to take out an ad, maybe? Put up a sign, 'Get your drugs here'?"

"Maybe I just don't want to live my life assuming everyone's guilty until proven innocent!"

"You'd be right more often than wrong."

For a long moment she just stared at him. And then, with a different sort of sadness than he'd seen before, she shook her head.

"Poor Jordy," was all she said.

And then she turned and walked away. Wyatt told himself it was just as well.

But still he watched. Watched the graceful, feminine walk, watched the fading sun fire her hair, watched as she got farther and farther away. And as her figure got smaller and smaller, the sense of loss inside him got bigger.

And no amount of telling himself you can't lose what you've never had seemed to help.

Chapter 12

She had, without a doubt, lost her mind.

With every step she took, Kai wondered. What on earth had possessed her to even try to reach that man? He was prickly, as her mom would say. And tense, wary, suspicious of everyone. Too hard on Jordy at a time when the boy needed some gentle understanding.

But he was also desperately trying to do the right thing. And he appeared to be just as hard if not harder on himself than he was on Jordy.

Not to mention lean, strong and sexy as hell, she thought, her mouth twisting into a annoyed grimace. *Oh, yeah, let's not forget that.*

As if she could forget. Just the way he moved

drew her eye, and the eyes that were striking
in Jordy were incredible in his father. They'd
be lethal if they weren't so exhausted and full
of mistrust. But perhaps that was all he knew,
thanks to his own father. Perhaps the only way
he could think of to protect his son was to distrust everyone around him.

By the time she got home, she was so annoyed with herself that she knew she was in
for a rough night if she didn't get some of this
out. So instead of going upstairs, she unlocked
the back door of the shop and went in. She
headed straight for the sound room and picked
up BeeGee.

She started right in with the most raucous
riffs she knew, loud, hammering, angry. She
knew how it would go; she would start with
this, concentrate on adding her own personal
twists to familiar patterns, and when she finally segued into calmer, smoother bits she
would be back under control and able to deal.
Other people worked out, some did yoga, some
practiced martial arts, but for her, this was
what worked.

It took her a while tonight. It was late when

she at last set the guitar down. But she was calm. Sad still, but calm. Enough to sleep anyway.

To her surprise, the next afternoon Jordy arrived at his usual time. She'd gotten the impression his grounding was going to go on much longer.

"I'm still grounded," he explained. "I can't go anywhere else. But…he's letting me come here."

Kai felt an odd sensation somewhere around her stomach. Was this a result of their conversation last night? Had he actually listened to her? She hadn't harped on it, just mentioned that he might regret using the music as a tool against his son, but…

"I have to come straight here after school, and stay here until he picks me up."

Jordy said it like a complaint, but his heart didn't seem to be in it, as if it were more reflex than genuine.

"So he can be reasonable," Kai said.

"Maybe," Jordy said, clearly unconvinced. It didn't matter, she had the feeling he'd said it as much for her as for him.

"Well, get started then," she said, with a gesture toward the back room.

Jordy nodded. "I have to make up for the days I missed."

"You won't have lost that much ground in three days," she promised him.

After the boy had closed the door behind him, Kai went back to unpacking the carton of picks and guitar straps that had arrived this morning. When it was emptied, she flattened the box and headed out back to put it in the Dumpster in the alley.

A few feet before she got to the outer door, she heard voices. Or rather a voice; one was loud enough to hear even through the closed doors, the other only presumed because the loud voice was talking to someone else. The closed fire door muffled the sounds so that she couldn't be sure of anything except that the voice she could hear was male.

When she pulled open the door it was like a camera suddenly focusing. And she realized two things immediately. The loud voice was Max, and it held that nasty, sneering tone she'd heard from him on occasion. Usually before he realized she was around and it turned back to that phony charm and sweetness. Second, she could now hear the second voice, low and steady. And thirdly, belatedly, she realized something else.

The other voice belonged to Wyatt Blake.

"—my son."

"It's a free country, I can hang with whoever I want."

"Whatever you're after, you're not using my son to get it. Stay away from him."

"Or what?" Max retorted, the sneer even more blatant.

Contrary to Max's loudness, Wyatt's voice got lower, quieter. Kai almost involuntarily edged forward, toward the corner of the Dumpster.

"Or I will make you wish you had."

Something about his tone, or perhaps that quietness, sent a shiver down Kai's spine. She'd never heard that voice from him before. She'd never heard a voice like that from *anyone*. And only a fool would not take heed.

But then, she'd always thought Max a bit of a fool.

Max laughed, a cocky, arrogant laugh. "Listen to the pill counter," he said.

Obviously she wasn't the only one Jordy whined about that to. But that didn't matter; there was something about not just Max's tone but his attitude, his body language, that had her worried. She wasn't sure what it was, or what she was afraid might happen, but—

And then it did happen. Or rather three things did, in rapid succession.

Max reached into his jacket pocket.

Almost simultaneously Wyatt's entire demeanor shifted as he drew up tight, looking wired, ready.

And Max's right hand came out of his pocket with a knife.

He flicked his wrist with a jerky sort of motion, then grabbed the split handle that opened up, revealing a deadly blade that had to be five inches long.

She gasped as he made a jab at Wyatt. Instinctively she took two more steps forward, although her common sense was telling her to get back inside and call the cops.

And then she stopped dead in her tracks,

staring in shock at what was unfolding less than thirty feet away.

Wyatt moved with a swiftness that made him practically a blur. She wasn't sure what he'd done, let alone how he'd done it. All she knew was that in barely over a second Max was face down on the asphalt, Wyatt above him with a knee pressed against his back around the kidneys.

Max was yelling, she guessed as much in shock as in pain. *She* was certainly shocked. It had been like some movie stunt, smooth, efficient and effective. She stared as Max struggled fruitlessly. He still held the knife, and flailed out wildly with it, trying to strike. Even as she thought it, Wyatt reached out with his right hand and captured Max's wrist.

He didn't seem to do anything else, just held the wrist. But Max's yelp of protest became a howl of pain. And after about three seconds, the knife clattered to the asphalt, dropped by apparently numbed fingers.

"Little children shouldn't play with sharp objects," Wyatt said.

She'd thought his voice intimidating before, but now it was worse. The only word she could think of was *frightening*. Not that she was frightened, it wasn't aimed at her after all, but still...

And the message finally got through to Max; he was down, trapped, unarmed, and finally, apparently listening.

"If you go near my son again, I will carve you up with your own knife."

It wasn't a threat, Kai thought, feeling almost numb. It wasn't a threat, wasn't even a promise. It was a flat, simple statement of fact that was infinitely more chilling than either.

As was the realization that in that moment, she was absolutely certain that Wyatt Blake would—and apparently could—back it up.

She'd brought this on, she thought in stunned shock. If she hadn't told Wyatt about Max... But she'd had to, she thought, quashing a tiny qualm of guilt. He was worried about Jordy, and rightfully so. If Max really was dealing drugs, then no right-thinking parent would want their child around him. *She* didn't want

Jordan around him, so she couldn't blame
Wyatt for taking action.

She'd just never expected *this* kind of action.

Wyatt got up in a smooth, fluid motion. Max
rolled over and scrabbled backward awkwardly,
like a crab missing a leg. She couldn't see
Wyatt's face, his back was to her. But she could
see the fear in Max's as he stared at the man.
Without a word he got slowly to his feet. His
eyes never left Wyatt. And whatever he was
seeing in Wyatt's expression kept him silent.
And after a moment's hesitation, he started
backing away. When he apparently felt safe
enough, he turned. And ran.

Kai let out a breath she hadn't even been
aware of holding. Became aware of the hammering of her heart in her chest, even as it
began to slow. The letdown was fierce, ener-
vating. But she still noticed his easy, heedless
proficiency, vastly smoother than Max's jerky
motion, as he flipped the knife closed, hiding
the deadly blade between the two halves of the
split handle.

And then, oddly, he went very still. Froze in
place, stiff, alert. Slowly, he turned around. No

surprise registered on his face, and she realized that somehow he had sensed she was there.

"Kai," he said.

"That's who I am," she said. "The question is, who the hell are you?"

Chapter 13

Wyatt slipped Max's butterfly knife into his pocket. He brushed off the left knee of his jeans. He picked up the bakery bag he'd set on a ledge when he'd first spotted Max headed for the back door of Play On. It contained a peace offering of sorts. He thought he might need it after the way she'd left the house last night. After the way he'd acted, blaming her for not telling him about Max sooner instead of thanking her for telling him at all.

The white bag held a jelly doughnut for Jordan—Melissa had told him the boy loved them, one of the long list of things she had rolled off in a desperate rush, knowing she didn't have much time—and some kind of cream cheese stuffed cinnamon roll for Kai, because Mrs. Day in the bakery had told him she had a weakness for them.

"Wyatt? Are you going to ignore me?"

He nearly laughed aloud. "If only I could."

She crossed her arms. "I understand you only talk to me because of Jordy. You don't have to be snarky about it."

He bit back the urge to apologize, to explain he hadn't meant it that way. At the same time, a little, self-preserving voice in the back of his head was yelling, *Let her think it, maybe she'll keep her distance. Safer.*

Safer for her, he couldn't deny that. People who got close to him ended up hurt. Or worse.

Sure. Wanting her at a distance had nothing to do with his own mental safety.

"Who are you, Wyatt?" she asked again. "Or rather, *what* are you?"

With an effort, he got a grip on his rocketing thoughts. "A pill counter, hasn't Jordan told you?"

"That," she said, with a gesture toward the alley where the altercation had occurred, "was not the move of a pill counter. What are you, some undercover cop or something?"

He laughed; he couldn't help it. It was a harsh, bitter sound even to himself. He wished it was that simple.

"I am just a boring guy with a son I never planned on, a son who hates me, a son I have no idea how to deal with."

But he'd known how to deal with Max. There hadn't been any hesitation; the location was good, the opportunity was there and he'd taken it. There was no good reason a man Max's age would pursue a friendship with a thirteen-year-old he wasn't related to. And that he was apparently the local drug supplier made immediate action imperative.

Kai studied him silently, long enough to make him uncomfortable. He changed the subject abruptly, not caring if it was obvious.

"Who's minding the store? Don't you need to get back inside?"

"That's the nice thing about Deer Creek. Most of the time most of the people are trustworthy, and you can leave your front door open safely."

But she turned toward the door despite her words.

"I suppose you don't put me in that group." Lord, what the hell was wrong with him, where had that come from?

She glanced back at him as he followed her, closing the back door behind them.

"Oh, I suspect you're eminently trustworthy yourself," she said, startling him. "Your problem is you don't trust anybody else. Including your own son."

I trust you.

Even as the unexpected—and completely unwanted—words formed in his head, he realized they were true. And the realization stunned him. But somehow, somewhere along the line, the impossible had become true.

He glanced at the closed door to the sound room. The hour wasn't up for another five minutes, and Jordan was obviously going to take advantage of every second.

"I trust you with Jordan," Wyatt said, adding the qualifier as if it could distance him from the revelation. "I know you've got his best interests at heart."

"I do."

Again she studied him for a silent moment, and he instinctively braced himself. One thing he really could trust her to do was to rattle his cage on a regular basis.

"Do you trust Mr. Hunt?"

"He's a good guy. A good boss."

"So, you trust him at work but not personally?"

"Moot point. There's nothing he can do to help with Jordan."

"Because he has only girls?"

Wyatt blinked. "Because it's my problem, not his."

"So you don't trust anyone completely, on all fronts."

"Everybody has their weak spots."

"Even you?"

"Especially me," he said, knowing his weakest spot was right now in that room a few feet away.

"Hmm."

He wondered what she was thinking, what the noncommittal sound meant, but didn't want to ask. He'd never intended for her—for anyone—to witness his encounter with Max, never would have pursued it if they hadn't been in the usually deserted alley. He had the unsettling feeling that those few seconds had changed her entire perception of him, and he wasn't sure what ramifications that might have.

"Speaking of problems," she said, "what if Max calls the cops on you for assault or something?"

"He won't."

"How can you be so sure?"

"Because I know the type. He won't want the police sniffing around him. He's afraid of what they might find."

She grimaced slightly, but didn't argue the point. She wasn't foolish, just…overly optimistic about people, he thought. True, he didn't trust anyone completely, but she trusted too many too completely. That might be a nicer way to live, but it also meant that when reality bit, it bit hard and fast and without warning. And sometimes lethally.

"I'm not late!"

Jordan's voice cut through the silence. Wyatt turned to look at his son, the boy who looked enough like he had at that age to make many of the locals who had been here then comment on it.

"Never said you were," Wyatt said mildly. Then he indicated the white bag. "Jelly doughnut in there for you."

Jordan looked only a little less than stunned. "What about it spoiling my dinner?"

"Dinner will be all vegetables to make up for it."

Jordan made a face, but he dug into the bag. Kai laughed. It was a light, silvery sound.

"Hey, Kai, there's a cream cheese roll in here, your favorite!"

"It's for her," Wyatt said. Kai gave him a look almost as stunned as Jordan's. "Mrs. Day told me you liked them."

She took the treat that Jordan handed her, but she was staring at him.

"Thank you," she said.

There was something in her voice, some quiet, almost husky undertone that made him speak hastily, a lame pushing of the already lame joke. "You can pass on the vegetables."

But she laughed again, and again it seemed

almost a physical thing, darting, wrapping around him. He had the crazy thought that if he sprayed beam visualizer in the air, it would be able to pick it out in the way it picked out the laser beams of an alarm system.

And your alarm system should be trumpeting, he thought.

"What about you?" she asked.

"What?"

She indicated the bag. "Did you already eat yours?"

"Oh. No."

"You don't indulge?"

"No."

She glanced at Jordan, who was intently wiping jelly from his chin, ignoring them both for the moment. She looked back at him.

"In anything?" she asked.

He couldn't say that her voice had changed, or even that she was looking at him any differently. But that didn't stop his pulse from kicking into high gear or heat from pooling somewhere low and deep inside him.

He wanted to say "never." Tried to say it. The word wouldn't come.

"Depends on the offer," was what came out instead. He was almost embarrassed to realize his voice sounded as thick and hot as his blood seemed to be at the moment. At any moment, when he was around this woman.

Get out of here, before you freaking overheat, he ordered himself. There was no room in his life for this, especially now. If there was trouble coming down the pike, he didn't want her anywhere around.

He expected Jordan to protest, but with the assurance that he could come back tomorrow he left compliantly enough.

Wyatt drove home, keeping one eye out for anything unusual. He couldn't put it out of the realm of possibility that Max might want retribution. He hoped not. As far as Max knew no one had witnessed his humiliation. If the kid had known Kai had seen it, he'd probably be waiting with a rocket launcher, Wyatt thought wryly.

Jordan was humming.

He risked a sideways glance at his son, afraid of disrupting the peace. There was a small, barely perceptible smile curving the usually sulky teenager's mouth.

Great, Wyatt thought. All it took was a jelly doughnut and a promise of getting tomorrow at Kai's. Simple. He should have thought of it before.

His mouth twisted wryly as he realized the formula would probably work on him, too.

Chapter 14

At first, after they'd left, Kai resisted the urge that had been growing in her since she'd seen Wyatt Blake take Max and his knife down with professional ease and efficiency. But she finally gave in, and pulled out her cell phone.

It had been a long time since she'd called the number. A long time since she'd called any number from that time. But she'd never deleted them, although they were long gone from her speed dial and this one she had to look up.

Once she found it, she hesitated anew. Not because she thought her call wouldn't be welcomed, she knew it would; David had been a good friend, and had understood her need to move on after Kit's death. He would be glad to hear from her.

She just didn't know if she wanted to take this step that seemed much bigger than a simple phone call. She felt as if she were standing on a mountain, trying to decide if she should start that snowball down.

But her curiosity, that same curiosity that had gotten her in trouble more than once as a kid, was raging full force now, so she made the call. Went through the usual niceties, then made her request. She wanted to know who Wyatt really was, wanted to know if her instincts were right, instincts that were screaming he was far more than just the pill counter he and his son both seemed determined to claim he was.

It was for Jordy's sake, of course. Not her own. It didn't really matter to her. It wasn't like it made any difference to her.

Depends on the offer....

Lord, the way he'd looked at her, the way he'd sounded nearly melted her bones.

Maybe that was her problem. Maybe that was why she'd made that call, she simply didn't want to admit a pill counter could send her senses reeling. Maybe she really was that shallow.

Question was, would whatever she found out make any difference? Or was she already in too deep with this man who fascinated her and annoyed her by turns? This man who could, based on what she'd seen, be dangerous. To Jordy. And to her.

She had a sinking feeling she already knew the answer.

"Dad?"

Wyatt froze, glad he was driving and had to keep his eyes on the road, so Jordan couldn't see his face. His son never called him "dad." To others, online and he was sure in person, he was just "my father," "old man" or simply the hated "him." Maybe names more foul. To his face, he didn't call him anything, only occasionally threw in an exaggerated "sir" that was nothing short of an insult in tone.

"What?" he asked, keeping his tone level, afraid if he commented on the appellation, made it a big deal, he'd never hear it again.

Maybe easing up, letting him go back to his

practice had been a good idea after all. He'd doubted it, had chided himself for giving in, told himself he was being an idiot, that he was letting Kai Reynolds get to him.

Oh, yeah, she gets to you, he thought now. *In a big way. A way you can't afford, especially right now.*

"—come from?"

He yanked himself back to the matter at hand, furious with himself that he'd let thoughts of the woman who was taking up far too much room in his head already, distract him from what seemed to be an overture of peace from his son.

"What do you mean?" he asked, hoping the boy would repeat his question.

Jordan gave him a sideways look, as if he was trying to decide if he was in trouble. For just asking a question? Maybe Kai was right, maybe he—

"I was just asking where all the stuff comes from. The pills and stuff you guys pack. And count."

He wanted to know how the detested pill counter counted? As a peace offering, it was odd, but he'd be a fool not to take it, he supposed.

"Several places," he answered. "Different plants make different things, ship them in bulk, and we take it from there."

"In bulk? Does that mean like…loose, like the bulk stuff at the market?"

"Exactly," he said, smiling at the apt comparison.

"And then those machines put it all in boxes?"

"In those annoying sheets you have to try and push them through, first, then into the boxes."

The faintest hint of a smile flickered on Jordan's face before he shifted his gaze away, staring down at a nub in the denim of his jeans, picking at the small imperfection with his thumb.

Wyatt didn't know what to think; Jordan had, until now, given less than a damn about his job. He'd like to believe the interest was genuine—although why it would be escaped him. After all, he'd intentionally gone after the most mind-numbing job he could find. And Jordan had openly despised it, belittled it and insulted him for having it.

He wanted to ask why the sudden interest, but he also didn't want to choke off the conversation. This was probably the most Jordan had said since he had handed him a permission slip for a field trip this Saturday, and had explained in a practiced paragraph what it was for.

"I know it seems boring, but it is important. Getting the right amount in the boxes, I mean."

"Sure."

Why did he have the feeling the boy had fought down a sarcastic answer?

"People get shorted, we hear about it." Jordan said nothing. He risked a question in turn. "What do you suppose happens if people get extra?"

The sideways look again. "I'll bet you don't hear about that."

"Exactly."

"So where do they keep the stuff, before it goes in the boxes?"

Wyatt blinked. "What?"

"The bulk stuff. Does it like come in big containers, or boxes they have to stick somewhere, or what?"

Wyatt hadn't, until that moment, realized

what he'd let happen. That he'd let hope, an emotion he'd thought himself through with long ago, build up. But now the alarm bells were going off like the days he'd thought left behind forever, as if he was back dealing with worst-case scenarios on a daily basis.

I should have known, he thought bitterly. *All this friendliness was more than a jelly doughnut could buy.*

The pieces tumbled together in the old way, and he saw the pattern he should have seen long ago. Max, the local drug dealer, befriends vulnerable young kid, acts as if he really likes him despite the age difference. Kid's father just happens to work at the local packaging plant. Which just happens to package an over-the-counter cold medication.

Which just happens to contain an ingredient used in brewing up the latest, most potent, deadliest form of methamphetamine to be found on the street.

And now that kid is asking questions he'd never asked before, about how the plant worked, and how and where the incoming product was stored.

The irony bit deep. Since they were a packaging plant, not a manufacturer or distributor, there wasn't much at HP in the way of security. In fact, once they'd realized how hot the product had become in illicit circles, John had wanted him to take over that security, heighten it, tighten it. He'd said no, not ready to leave the mind-numbing sameness of the job he had now.

And in the process, he'd opened the door to disaster.

Chapter 15

"Why the sudden interest? I thought you thought I have the most boring job in the world."

He tried to keep his tone neutral, but Jordan stiffened up anyway. "You don't think it's boring?"

"Sure it is. That's what I want."

For a long moment, as he maneuvered the car into the garage and shut the big door behind them, Jordan just sat there and looked at him. Wyatt just waited; he could tell by the boy's expression that the question hovering was going to burst loose at any moment. And it did.

"Why?"

"This job is fine. It pays the bills."

"Don't you *want* a better job?"

"No."

"If you had a better job, maybe I could have texting on my phone."

For a moment Wyatt felt a stab of doubt. Was that what all this was really about for Jordan, he wanted something and thought if he showed an interest he might get it? Did it really have nothing to do with Max at all?

Maybe his instincts had gotten rustier than he thought in the past year.

Or maybe it was just that he had no parenting instincts at all.

"You're surviving without it," he said.

"Great," Jordan muttered, getting out of the SUV and slamming the door shut.

Of course, the fact that Jordan had a cell phone with very few call minutes on it, for emergencies only and no texting or internet, had been intentional, not because of finances. He'd done it thinking that eventually, if things improved, he would indeed upgrade the boy's plan.

But a couple of questions on the pretext of

showing an interest in his work didn't accomplish that.

He stood in front of the door into the house, blocking it without being obvious about it. And as Jordan came to a halt in front of him, he repeated his initial question.

"So why? You've never cared about my work before."

Jordan didn't even look up at him. "I was just curious, all right? Can we go in? I've got homework."

Like you're always in a hurry to get to that, Wyatt thought.

"Then go get started," he said. "We'll hold dinner until you're done."

"Vegetables? I'll pass," Jordan said with a grimace.

"That was a joke, Jordan," he said quietly.

"Oh. Ha."

There was, he supposed, no sarcasm in the world like that of a teenager. That at least he remembered from his own days of throwing it at his own father. And those memories kept him from reacting the way his own father had; he merely repeated the instruction to get started on that homework.

Once Jordan was settled in he went to the kitchen. He'd never been much of a cook, his life wasn't conducive to it. Or at least, it hadn't been. Now he was a fair hand with the basics, but that was it.

Maybe he should really do the vegetables, he thought, blessing the person who'd invented the microwave-in-the-bag process. One huge plate of whatever was in the freezer.

He knew he was avoiding what he should be thinking about. But he had to make a decision, and he didn't have the information he needed to make the right one. He didn't know the most crucial thing, the most important piece. If his instincts were right, he had to know how deep Jordan was in.

What would a normal guy who suspected what he suspected do? Call the cops, of course. But that normal person would probably have a normal relationship with his kid. And the kid would, even with the usual rebellion, likely trust him, at the core.

Jordan did not trust him. At all. And if there

was nothing else he'd learned in his checkered life, it was that you couldn't force trust.

He pondered the dilemma. If he pushed, Jordan would just clam up again, like he had in the garage. And that would not only tell him nothing, it might inspire Jordan to warn Max that he was suspicious.

He should warn John. He would understand, and he knew enough to put credence in Wyatt's suspicions. But again, he couldn't risk it; what if Jordan was deeper into this than just as a source for Max to pump? He could be, lured by the false friendship offered by Max. The boy wasn't using, he was almost certain of that. He did regular searches, and knew too well all the signs to look for. But he wouldn't put it past someone like Max to try and hook the boy, get him desperate enough for the drugs to do whatever he had to to keep the supply coming.

Including providing information.

You don't trust anybody else. Including your own son.

Kai's words echoed in his head. He'd known they were true at the time, but right now they were even more prescient.

Kai.

Jordan talked to Kai. He trusted her.

Wyatt sighed. Grimaced. Shook his head, feeling helpless. It wasn't a sensation he'd felt often, and he certainly didn't care for it.

Finally he faced the inevitable. He couldn't put his confused feelings above Jordan's welfare. He couldn't avoid the best chance he had at getting the information he needed to keep his son safe.

He was going to have to go to Kai for help.

She looked up when he came in. He glanced up at the speaker over the door, where the last notes of today's welcome faded. She'd even gotten him wondering every time he came in, which he guessed meant it was working.

"Chaos Creek," she said when he got close enough, answering before he could ask.

He blinked. "What?"

She laughed. "The Johnsons' son's band. They won the battle this summer at the county fair, so I thought I'd change the rotation and feature them. Local boys made good and all."

"They sound good."

"They are. He was happy to come in and lay down some riffs for me." She grinned. "Not to mention he and his band and all their friends have been coming in all week just to hear it. And shop. I should have thought of it sooner."

He suspected the appeal was a bit more than just hearing the band play when the door opened and closed. But then, he was perhaps a bit biased. When you couldn't get a woman out of your head, you tended to assume other men felt the same. Even teenagers.

Maybe especially teenagers.

"You're good at this."

"Yes," she said simply. He liked that. Then she lifted a brow at him. "You're early. Jordy's just getting started."

"I know. I needed to talk to you. About him."

For a moment she just looked at him, assessingly. "Serious stuff?" she finally asked.

He nodded. To his surprised, she slid off the stool behind the counter, walked to the front door, locked it and flipped the open sign over so that the closed side showed in the door. It touched him in a very odd and unexpected

way, that she accepted the serious part so un-
questioningly.

"You want some coffee? I've got some upstairs. We can leave Jordy a note to come up
when he's done."

He knew she lived over the store. That es-
sentially she was inviting him into her home.
Necessity warred with panic, leavened by curiosity about what her place would look like.

*What are you going to do, jump her the
minute you've got her alone?*

Not, he thought ruefully, an unwelcome
thought. He'd been alone and done without too
long, he thought, when his mind took a nosedive into places it didn't belong at the slightest
provocation.

Necessity and curiosity won out over his
unease about being with her in her personal
space. He wasn't sure what he expected as he
followed her up the stairs, but what he saw
when they stepped inside wasn't it. Her apartment was open, spacious, with comfortable fur-
niture arranged to make the most of the large
room, and sparsely but effectively adorned

with pieces of bright blue and deep green, mirroring the landscape outside on a clear day.

The kitchen appeared to have been updated, opened up into the main room. He took a seat on one of the barstools pulled up to the granite counter, and watched as she set the coffee machine to working.

As it began to drip, she turned to face him.

"I like your place," he said.

"It works well for me."

"Close to work."

"Can't get much closer. I can run up during the day, and I've got a buzzer rigged if somebody comes into the store."

"Handy."

"Yes. Between it and the store, it was more than I wanted to spend, but it's been worth it."

He blinked. "You own it? The whole building?"

She laughed. "You make it sound like a skyscraper. But I own all two floors, yes."

She'd surprised him yet again.

"What if you decided you hated it here?"

She didn't say it, but the look she gave him said "Like you did?" as clearly as if she had.

But then, she hadn't grown up here, under the watchful eyes of...everyone.

"I knew I'd love it, and I do. Now that it's fairly stable, I have to make sure I leave the work behind at the end of the day, though."

"Do you succeed?"

"Most of the time. It's an effort, though. It would be easy to stay as consumed by it as I was in the beginning."

"Don't."

"Voice of experience?"

"Yes."

She only nodded, as if she'd suspected as much. He watched as she glanced at the now half-full coffee pot. Then she turned back to him.

"Did you notice Jordy was really edgy today?" she asked.

His mouth quirked. "How could I tell? He's always edgy around me."

She smiled at him. "There is that," she said, and he liked that she didn't deny it, or try to reassure him with some meaningless platitude. "Any idea what might have him so wound up?"

"Maybe."

She studied him for a moment. "That's what you wanted to talk to me about."

It wasn't a question, and she didn't go on. She reached into a cupboard and pulled out two mugs, one blue, one green. Waited as the stream of coffee diminished, then stopped, then filled the mugs.

"Black?" she asked.

He nodded. She slid the blue one toward him on the counter, then added a spoonful of sugar to her own mug. She took a sip, wrapping her hands around the mug as if savoring the heat. And that quickly, his mind was taking that nosedive again.

"I suggest you just dive in," she said.

He nearly choked on his swallow of coffee at her choice of words. It took him a second to convince himself there was no way she could know where his mind had wandered.

He took another swallow of coffee, to ease his throat and marshal his thoughts. And in the end, he took her advice and simply laid it all out for her, Jordan's sudden interest in his job, the specifics of his questions, and his own suspicions.

To his surprise, she accepted it all.

"It makes sense," she said when he asked. "I always knew Max was up to something. I just didn't know—or didn't want to know—exactly what."

"About that," he began, uncomfortable about what he'd yelled at her that day.

She shook her head, cutting him off. "You were right. I should have told you my suspicions right away. For Jordy's sake. If he is caught up in this…"

"And that's what I need to know. But he won't talk to me." He hesitated. *Just dive in....* "But he does talk to you."

She stared at him for a long moment. He wondered how anyone could handle that intense gaze for long. Realized belatedly that that was the same thing people had once said about him.

"I need your help," he said, his voice low and harsh.

Many would have had a smart comment to make to that, or at least would have asked him how much it hurt to have to ask. Kai did neither.

"You want me to try and get him to tell me what he knows?" she asked.

"I have to know how deep he's in, to know what to do. How to protect him."

He half expected her to say no. To consider what he was asking was a betrayal of the boy's trust. At the least he expected to have to do some heavy convincing.

"All right. I'll try."

He blinked. "You will?"

"Yes."

He couldn't help himself, the question burst out. "Why?"

"Because if you're right, Jordy's in danger of getting sucked up into my worst nightmare."

It didn't take any special perception to understand where that had come from.

"Kit," he said softly.

She nodded. "That photograph in the store," she began.

"Etched in my memory," he said, then wished he hadn't. For a guy who didn't believe in wishing, he'd been doing a lot of it lately, he thought sourly.

"It's not there just to feed my ego. It's there to remind me."

"Remind you?"

"That night was the beginning of the end. The night I realized Kit was going to die, and probably soon." She sighed. "I did everything I could think of. I rallied friends and family to intervene, I threatened to leave, and actually did, for a while. Nothing worked."

"He wouldn't clean up, even for you?"

"Oh, he'd talk a good game, but he always slipped back. Finally I literally tricked him into rehab, told him we were just taking a much needed break from the road until the last second."

"So he didn't go of his own accord."

"No. Which explains why his sobriety lasted exactly six hours after he left the facility. He never forgave me for tricking him into it. But I loved him. I had to try."

And Kai Reynolds would always try, he thought.

She took a deep breath as if to steady herself before going on.

"Unfortunately, he loved alcohol and drugs more than he loved me. Or himself."

She said it without self-pity or anger, just that sadness.

"I'm sorry. For you being hurt."

"Caring costs," she said simply.

"He was a fool." *Don't you be one,* he ordered himself.

For a moment she just looked at him. Then, softly, she said, "Thank you."

"He had everything, and he threw it away."

"Yes."

"He had…you."

"Yes."

He couldn't seem to shut up, no matter how hard he tried. "Then he was worse than a fool."

She stared at him then, her eyes flicking over his face as if she were trying to read him. She'd always done pretty well at that before, so he wondered that what he was thinking wasn't as clear as a glowing neon sign to her.

Maybe because it's as clear as mud to you, he thought.

He hadn't felt anything like this in longer than he could remember. Maybe he never had, and that was why it felt so strange, so foreign, so overwhelming.

He set down his coffee mug. He took the single stride across the kitchen floor to her. Slowly, giving her every chance to stop him, he took her mug and set it on the counter behind her.

Close now, so close he could feel her warmth, as if it were a physical thing wrapping around him, welcoming, comforting, supporting. He cupped her face with his hands, hands he was surprised weren't shaking. His entire body had awakened in a rush, and the intensity was all the more startling because of how long it had been.

At least, that's what he told himself.

"Kai," he said, his voice a low, harsh, unfamiliar thing. "Stop me."

What the hell are you doing? he asked himself, not sure if he meant being about to kiss her or asking her to stop him.

She didn't. She just looked up at him, those gray eyes wide and dark.

Somewhere, some part of his mind was warning him he was messing with the one person who might get through to his son. And he realized with a little shock that he knew, somehow, that she would never jettison Jordan because of anything stupid his father did.

He trusted her on that.

It was the last coherent thought he had before he kissed her.

Chapter 16

Curiosity killed the cat.

Wasn't that how the old saying went? Kai was learning the truth of it now.

She'd never felt anything like this. And she certainly had never expected it from this man. Although to be honest, she'd been curious from the day he'd first walked into Play On. And now, when he'd finally made a move, she had been too curious about what it would be like to stop him.

She'd never expected him to…envelop her like this. To take charge of her senses, her pulse, her entire body, and send them all reeling out of control. Even in the wildness of youth, when she'd been crazy in love with Kit—or the idea of him—it hadn't been like this. So how could she have expected such a consuming heat?

Of course, she'd never expected him to actually make a move at all. Maybe that was it, she thought, a little dizzily. She was going all female and mushy because she knew he hadn't wanted to do this, but had done it anyway. Female power, all that.

And then his mouth moved on hers, tasting, probing and searing. And she realized the power wasn't hers, it wasn't even his; it was something generated by the combination, by the connection between the two of them. She wondered that she couldn't hear it crackle.

She kissed him back, not simply because she was unable not to, although it was true, but because she wanted to. She wanted more, more of that heat, that luring taste of him, more of the unexpected sweetness behind the gruff, sometimes intractable exterior.

She had the fleeting thought that breaking through that tough exterior made this all the more incredible. All the more precious. People valued things that were hard to get, her father had always said. Maybe he was right in more ways than she'd known.

And then she couldn't think at all. It was as if her system had no room for anything but the flood of physical sensations it was registering. As if there was nothing left in her entire world except this man, and the feel of his mouth on hers, his body pressed against hers, fierce and demanding and impossibly hot.

When at last he broke the kiss, she took what seemed to be her first breath in hours. It was an audible, gasping sound that only added to her shock. He didn't pull away, he was still pressed against her, knee to shoulder, and she thought she might whimper if he broke that contact, too.

He was staring down at her, brow furrowed, looking, not satisfied but almost…bewildered.

I know the feeling, she thought.

"What the hell was that?" His question came out as a whisper that nevertheless seemed to vibrate in the air.

She could think of several answers, most of them provocative, but her mouth didn't seem to want to work. The only thing it wanted was his back where it had been. Kissing her again. Stoking that fire again. Melting her again.

"Wonderful?" she finally suggested.

She heard him suck in a breath. He opened his mouth as if to speak, then stopped. Tried again. Finally, with an expression she could only describe as rueful, he lowered his head, shaking it in a way that matched the bewildered expression he'd worn moments ago.

"Kai, I…."

"You what?"

"Hell. I don't know."

"This could…complicate things," she said. "With Jordy, I mean."

His head came up. "Even if you're mad at me, you won't take it out on him."

She knew him well enough by now to realize the implications of his words. The simple fact that he trusted her not to do that was amazing. Perhaps intractable wasn't the word after all.

But that wasn't what she chose to answer; she doubted he'd talk about it anyway.

"Why would you think I'm mad at you?"

He took a half step back then, letting go of

her, breaking the last physical contact between them. It was all she could do not to protest aloud.

Especially when she realized, as the last of the pleasant haze lifted, that he had been as swamped by this as she had been; he didn't even try to hide the fact that he was thoroughly aroused.

Not that he could have, she thought, still a little off balance.

"I know you didn't want…that."

It wasn't an apology, but it was close enough to spark a bit of the remaining fire in her. She crossed her arms, as much to steady herself as anything, and looked at him levelly.

"I am a fully grown, adult woman," she said. "I'm quite capable of making my preferences crystal clear."

He blinked.

"If I hadn't wanted 'that,' you would have known it."

One corner of his mouth twitched upward. "Why do I get the feeling that I'd be wearing your hot coffee?"

Again that flash of humor made her wonder

what he must have been like before...before what? Before Jordy had landed on him? Or had he been this way much longer? When had his view of life changed?

A life, she reminded herself, she knew very little about. And wondered if he, like her, had had a single moment when things became vividly clear and undeniable, a moment that changed everything.

"I didn't mean to...complicate things," he said.

"There's a teenager involved. They were already complicated," Kai retorted.

But despite her joking, she knew he was right. Things had gotten even more complicated. Because she was about to, at least in Jordy's eyes, betray him completely. And she wasn't sure which the boy would think was worse; her trying to pry information out of him for his father, or her having the hots for that father.

Because you most certainly do, she thought; never had she responded to anyone like that, swift and fire-fierce. Even with Kit it seemed almost tame compared to this. At first she thought that impossible, but now that she could think again, she realized that she shouldn't be surprised. With Kit, she'd always been part of the music, and it was the music that got his full and total focus. After he'd died, she'd often wondered if they would have even been together if they hadn't shared that. And in her cooler, more analytical moments, she'd wondered if he would have looked twice at her if she hadn't been able to serve the music.

No one had ever focused on *her* the way Wyatt Blake just had. As if she were the only person in the world of any importance to him. As if she were some irresistible force that he, a strong, determined man, was unable to resist.

And he kissed her as if she were the oasis after an eon spent in the desert.

She nearly shuddered just at the memory. And she knew that despite everything, this was not something she wanted to run away from. She didn't think she even could.

And if she lined up every man in the town of Deer Creek—heck, the whole county—she doubted she could have picked a more difficult one to deal with.

Quite a knack she seemed to have.

* * *

If he'd had his way, he'd have sent Jordan to bed at seven o'clock, just so he could have time to think. But as it was, while Jordan was doing his homework on the computer in the den, then through the mostly silent meal, and after when Jordan was back on the computer, Wyatt had to fight off a flood of images and thoughts.

Jordan was still casting wary glances over his shoulder, as he had been ever since Wyatt sat down in the armchair a few feet away. He had a book in his hands, but he knew it was just an excuse; focusing on written text was beyond him at the moment. But he could stare at it as if he were reading, which was less obvious than staring into space.

He had to have been out of his mind. He'd gone this long without kissing, hell, without even touching a woman, so why now? Why at the worst possible time, when he should be focused entirely on Jordan? And why with the worst possible woman, one he had to rely on to help him keep Jordan safe, and get him away from the likes of Max Middleton?

If he could just categorize her in the old way,

as an asset, someone to be used to achieve the goal, then maybe he could keep his head on straight.

Keep? Yeah, right. Like your head isn't still spinning.

The last time he'd gotten this tangled up had resulted in Jordan. But he'd had a weak sort of excuse then; he'd been young, caught up in it all, and so damned full of himself. Life and his work hadn't thrashed all that out of him yet.

So how had he ended up here, at a time when he should be focused on just one thing, his son, seemingly unable to focus on anything but one woman? And worse, the one woman he most needed on his side? Every working brain cell told him he should back off, that he didn't dare risk that he would, as he usually did, screw things up.

Then again, there was nothing usual about what he was feeling. Even the flash fire of youth and foolishness that had resulted in the boy sitting a few feet away had been nothing compared to this.

It was all he could do not to reach up and touch his own mouth, where he could swear he could still feel the softness, the warmth, the very shape of her lips.

He suppressed a shudder at the memory, tamped down his body's eager response to just the remembered feel and taste of her. When it had been the real thing, when she had been in his arms and his mouth had been on hers, it had been nearly unbearable. And no amount of telling himself he'd simply gone too long without could explain the explosiveness of his response.

He couldn't believe that last month this time, she'd been only a name to him. And now he seemed to be carrying her around with him; she was in his head all the time. Even the soothing anodyne of his job hadn't been enough to keep her at bay; he caught himself thinking of her at the oddest times.

And now you've really done it, he told himself. Now he had even more insistent and fierce images to fight off. And he wasn't doing a very good job of it.

"I know you're not reading, not really."

He blinked, and looked up. Jordan was standing there, a couple of feet away. And he'd been so entranced by those overheated visions in his head that he hadn't even realized the boy had gotten up from the computer. That shocked him fully back into the present.

"You haven't turned a page in forever."

He didn't deny it. "Having a little trouble concentrating tonight."

He waited, wondering if Jordan was going to broach the subject again, try to pump him for information he could pass along to Max. Wondered what Max would do if approached, after their little encounter. He'd scared him then, he knew, but time had passed, and Max's cocky self-assurance would slowly flow back; he knew the type.

It hadn't come up with Jordan again since last night, but he doubted it was over. If for no other reason than Max wasn't likely to give up. He'd just make sure Wyatt never found out there'd been any contact. He wondered what kind of pressure the young dealer was putting on the boy.

If things were normal, he would simply apply his own kind of pressure to get Jordan to tell him. But if he did that, if he resorted to the old

ways, there wouldn't be any kind of relationship left when he was done.

Like it's so great now?

No, he admitted silently to that nagging little
voice, but he didn't want to destroy what little
there was.

Fleetingly, as his son stared down at him,
obviously working up to saying something, he
wondered what the boy would do if he knew
what his father and his beloved Kai had been
up to while he'd been practicing. Wondered
how he'd feel if he knew his father was sitting
here wishing with every aching cell in his body
that it had gone further.

Wishing that, despite the fact that it would ir-
revocably complicate every aspect of his life,
that it would go much further. He wanted to see
the bedroom in that airy, comfortable apartment, and he wanted to see it soon.

From the bed.

Next to her.

On top of her.

In her.

And he nearly groaned aloud at the swift,

wickedly hot clench of his body at the mere thought of it.

"Never mind," Jordan said abruptly and turned away, telling Wyatt something had shown in his face. Probably pain, he thought wryly. There was another skill that had apparently gotten rusty; time was he'd been able to hide any thoughts at all.

But then, he didn't think he'd ever had thoughts like this to hide.

"Jordan, wait." It was becoming an effort, the more he was around Kai, to not call him Jordy. But even if he knew little else, he knew that permission had to come from his son. "I was caught up in another problem."

Jordan looked back at him. "That's all I am to you, isn't it? A problem."

Wyatt mentally kicked himself for his choice of words; he couldn't seem to do anything right with this boy. He'd handled what most would consider much bigger problems than one teenager's moods with cool efficiency, but here he was at a loss.

Caring costs.

Kai's words echoed in his head. She knew

the truth of them, better than many people ever did. Yet she still let herself care. It probably never occurred to her to try not to. And for the first time in his life he saw the simple, honest courage in that.

"You scare me," he said to his son. "And that's a problem, yes."

"I scare you?" Jordan sounded astonished. But he came back, clearly wanting an explanation.

"Your mother knew what to do," he said. "Sometimes I think women know instinctively."

It was the first time in months they'd even spoken about Melissa, although as little as they'd spoken at all, it wasn't surprising.

"She was the best," Jordan said, his voice tight.

"I know you miss her. I know you wish she was here, not me. So do I, for both our sakes. But she's not. We're all we've got."

"You didn't even love her."

"No. And she didn't love me."

They'd decided not to lie about that. Melissa had always told Jordan that it didn't matter, because out of what had been an impulse of the moment had come the thing she loved most: him. To her credit, she'd never tried to belittle the cost of that impulse, but she'd also managed to never make Jordan feel unloved because of it.

A knack he didn't seem to have.

"I know I'm not good at being a parent, not like your mom. But I care too much not to try."

Jordan blinked. "You don't care."

"If I didn't, I wouldn't be here."

"Why *are* you here?" Jordan's voice rose, and Wyatt guessed his emotions were rising with it. "You didn't love my mom, you don't love me."

He didn't know how to answer that. He never had. And now, with his emotions so tangled and confused, he knew even less. So the only words that came out were blunt, simple, and at least true.

"You're mine."

Oddly, the two-word answer seemed to derail the building storm. Jordan's glare faded, and he lowered his gaze.

"What did you want?" Wyatt asked.

The boy's head came up. "I want to download some music."

It wasn't a huge leap to figure out whose. "Kai's band?"

He nodded. "She gave me their first CD to rip, but I want to buy the rest. The last one, especially."

The masterpiece, that music blogger had called it, Wyatt remembered. "Don't want to cheat her out of the money? That's a good thought, Jordan."

He shifted his feet as if embarrassed. "She gives it away anyway. All the money from their music goes to the rehab center she started."

"I know." Jordan blinked, surprised. "But you don't have to download it. Not the last one, anyway."

"I'll pay back the money. I'll do extra work around here, whatever."

Well, that had to mean he was serious, Wyatt thought ruefully.

"You can do that for the other CD. But the last one…it's already there."

Jordan blinked. "What?"

"It's in the music folder."

Jordan stared at him, clearly stunned. "You?"

"Hard to believe, huh?"

"Did you…listen?"

"Repeatedly." And he had, from the time he'd downloaded it, that night after she'd come here and he'd made her so angry she walked away. "It really is a masterpiece."

Jordan looked utterly flummoxed. And for the first time since their lives had collided, Wyatt felt a sense of amused satisfaction.

"Tough call, isn't it?" he said. "Do you now hate it because I like it, or do you go along with the guy you already hate?"

Loyalty won out, and quickly. "It's Kai. I could never hate it."

"Good for you. Right decision."

Wyatt kept his tone level, but inside he was pleased.

Later, after Jordan had transferred the music to his small player and retreated up to his room to listen before bed, Wyatt took his place at the computer. He got out the headphones, put them on and made himself go through the usual checks. Except for the flurry of expected angry explanations of why he hadn't shown up the other night, the postings on Jordan's networking page had slowed down a lot since he'd been practicing at Play On. Another benefit, Wyatt thought.

There was no post at all today, and no new messages. Satisfied that that front was handled, he was about to shut down when the alert window popped up again.

He jumped through the hoops until he was reading the newest message. He supposed to some the fact that the inquiries on his whereabouts had seemingly ceased days ago would be a relief. To some, it would be proof that whoever it was had given up.

To Wyatt Blake, it meant they'd found him.

Chapter 17

Wyatt sat with his hands wrapped around the coffee mug. And he would keep his hands right there. Think of it as a deadman detonator, he told himself. You let go of it, and you blow everything to bits.

He sensed Kai's gaze on him as if it were a physical thing. As if by the mere act of looking at him she could set nerve endings tingling in places he couldn't quite ignore.

For days now they'd done this—it was in danger of becoming a habit—decamping to her apartment while Jordan practiced. He'd felt guilty about her leaving the store, but so far, only twice had she had to go back downstairs to handle a customer who'd rung the buzzer. Still, every day he'd told himself he'd wait until four-thirty to go pick the boy up. And every day he was there within minutes after the sound room door had closed on the budding musician.

"We have progress," Kai said after a sip from her own mug of coffee.

They did? He didn't feel that way. He felt in limbo, wanting more than anything to revisit that crazed, wild place he'd fallen into at the first touch of her lips, yet afraid of what might happen if he did.

Wyatt looked up from his hands. "Progress?" he asked, tentatively.

"I listened to a bit he recorded last night. He's sounding better."

Wyatt felt like a fool. She meant Jordan, of course. Idiot. He jerked himself out of the stupid reverie he'd let himself drift into, thinking about kissing and more and the fact that her bedroom was mere yards away.

"Anything that sounds like actual music yet?"

She laughed. "Well, since there's a pretty

wide range of what various people consider music, I'd say the answer to that is yes. Sort of. More than before, anyway."

"Okay. Progress."

"Speaking of which, if you're expecting me to make any on...that other front, I'm going to need some time with him. More than five or ten minutes as he's coming or going, anyway."

He gave her a sideways look. She had told him earlier that there hadn't been any sign of Max since the day he'd told him to stay away from Jordan. She hadn't even seen him, or his friends, at the usual pizza hangout. He would like to think his warning had taken root. But he'd like to think whoever had been looking for him had given up, too. And newly reawakened instincts told him otherwise on both.

He'd warned John, and the man had agreed to two new temporary security guards, but it was going to take a couple of days to get that in place. Wyatt was regretting now that he hadn't made it clear to Max that he suspected what he was up to, but his only goal at the time had been keeping him away from Jordan.

"You have a plan?" he asked.

"I was thinking you might need to be late tomorrow. To pick him up, I mean."

He thought about it a moment, then nodded. "Okay," he said. "That will give you time alone with him."

She nodded in turn. "I think I can get him to hang around here and wait."

He nearly laughed. "You could get any male breathing to hang around."

She went very still. "Was that an assessment of my powers of discrimination?"

He frowned, not understanding. "What?"

"You seemed to think I once had none."

Sexy girl rocker....

His own thoughts came back to him, and he supposed he had once thought that, made assumptions that sex, drugs and rock and roll was more than just a saying.

He didn't try to dissemble. She was too perceptive, and he didn't want to risk denying something she obviously knew was true.

"I was wrong," he said simply. "About a lot of things. Very wrong."

She didn't seem surprised as much as pleased by the admission. Not in an "I win" sort of way, but more like he'd done the right thing by honestly admitting it, and that made her happy.

The idea that he had even the slightest power to make her happy hit him like a punch to the gut.

"Thank you," she said. And then, giving him a level look that somehow put him on guard, she added, "So, there's something I've been wondering."

"What?"

"Are you ever going to kiss me again?"

If the mug he held hadn't been heavy, thick stoneware, he thought it would have shattered under his sudden tension.

"Kai," he said, unsure if it was plea or warning.

"I mean, aren't you curious?"

The mug hit the counter. Coffee sloshed. "Curious? Is that what you call it?"

"I just meant, what it felt like...what if it was a fluke?"

He stood up, backed away from her, as if any kind of distance was safe when she had in fact taken up residence in his head.

"Yeah, it was such a fluke my brain's been

fried ever since. Such a fluke I can't get the visions of it out of my mind, can't focus, can't concentrate, can't—"

He broke off before he committed the total idiocy of telling her about the dreams. He'd wished for so long to be rid of the nightmares, but he'd never expected them to be replaced by hot, erotic images involving the most unlikely woman he could ever have imagined.

Careful what you wish for.

Truer words never spoken, he thought.

She was smiling at him. "Thank you," she said again, a soft huskiness in her voice that sent the same shivers through him that those dreams had.

But his brow furrowed; her words made no sense to him. And again she understood perfectly, as if she could read his mind.

"Nice to know I'm not alone."

He blinked. "Alone?"

Her mouth quirked. "Same problems."

He sucked in a breath that was so audible he knew she must have heard it even from five feet away, a distance that no longer seemed safe at all.

"I thought it was just me," he said.

She let out a compressed chuckle that sounded half frustrated, half wry amusement. He knew the feeling.

"I don't think it explodes like that going only one way," she said.

"I don't know. I've never felt an explosion like that before."

She smiled again. And it damned near took his breath away.

"We did a song once, called 'Playing With Fire.'"

"I know."

He'd surprised her that time. "You do?"

"It's on the last CD. One of the best on it, and that's saying something."

"Thank you, for the third time," she said. "I didn't realize you'd…listened."

"I'm trying to get better at listening," he said, and knew by her expression that she understood all the levels he meant that on.

"That song…that's what this feels like. To me."

He thought of the chorus, that line about

always going back to the flame because you're helpless not to. Yeah, it felt that way, all right.

"So, are you going to?"

"No."

She drew back a fraction. Looked at him for a long moment, as if he were a puzzle she was trying to find the key to. Then, slowly, she smiled.

"So it's my turn?"

God, she *could* read his mind. "Exactly."

He couldn't explain why, couldn't understand himself and why it was so important to him that she make the move. Yes, it was knowing that she wanted this, that he wasn't pushing her somewhere she didn't want to go, but it was more. He just wasn't sure what.

The only thing he was sure of was that he had to know if it had really been that hot, or if his imagination, over-energized by lack of exercise in that area, had built the memory of that single kiss into something reality could never match.

And then she was there, stepping into his arms. She tilted her head back, stretched up, brushed her lips tentatively over his.

And he realized he'd handed her the detonator, and she'd triggered the inferno without a second thought.

Chapter 18

Any thought that the first kiss had been a fluke was seared out of Kai's mind the moment her mouth touched his. For a bare few seconds, maybe three, he held back, letting her do the coaxing. But then a choked groan broke from him and he was kissing her back, fiercely, hotly.

She wondered vaguely if knowing what it *could* feel like influenced what it *did* feel like. Not that it mattered. What mattered was that she'd never felt anything like this before, not even in the frantic days with Kit. No, this was more, far more, something white-hot and consuming.

She clung to him as he seemed to sap the strength from her; any more and she'd be sagging weakly against him. And then he flicked his tongue over her lips, asking, and she parted for him without hesitation. She wanted, needed the taste of him, the hot, male, coffee-tinged taste of him more than she wanted her next breath.

He cupped her face as he invaded, and for a moment she just savored the feel of it, savored the tension in him, the low, harsh sound that she could both hear and feel deep in his chest.

She slid her hand down his back, wanting him closer. Her fingers traced the contours of lean, solid muscle; for a pill counter he was in great shape. She reached his waist, tightened her embrace, drawing him in. Any doubt she might have had that it was the same, instant conflagration for him was erased when she felt the prod of his erection against her and heard his low groan as they were pressed together chest to knee.

His hands moved downward as hers had, drawing them even closer, harder together. But then they slipped upward, to slowly, gently, cup the outer curves of her breasts. She shivered, drawing back just enough to give him more access; denial wasn't in her vocabulary with this man, it seemed. Not with this man.

For a moment he simply held her, letting the soft flesh mold to his hands. But then his thumbs brushed over nipples that were already taut and aching for just that, and she moaned softly, unable to stop the sound and not caring.

She was lost in the swirling sensations, and was thinking, crazily, that she was glad she'd made her bed this morning. She tugged at his shirt, wanting to feel the heat of him skin to skin, wanting to touch, wanting the feel of his hands on her own skin, wanting more, wanting…everything.

She returned the probing exploration of his tongue, thrilling at the way his breath caught, then stopped as she traced the even curve of his teeth, then beyond. He allowed her the invasion, welcomed it with a slide of his tongue over hers, and—

He stopped.

He not only stopped everything, leaving her

bereft, but went suddenly still and rigid in an entirely different way.

"Jordan," he said, in the same moment that she heard the clatter on the stairs from the store. Usually they were back downstairs before Jordy finished; not today.

They backed apart, as if it were instinctive. They hadn't talked about this, specifically, what to tell Jordy, if anything, about what had sprung to life between them. It was too new, too tentative, and too hotly private to share with anyone, but especially his son.

Besides, what if it's so hot it burns itself out? she thought.

"Kai," he began.

"We'll talk about it later," she said as a rapid, excited-sounding knock came on the door. Jordy had been up here once before, when he'd come up to get the CD she'd given him. He'd burst right in that day, and she was thankful now that she'd made the point that this was her home, not just an extension of her workplace, and that a knock on the door was required.

She tugged on her T-shirt to straighten it. He tucked his back in, hastily. Then he went back to the bar and picked up what had to be a cold cup of coffee by now; although if it was boiling from the heat they'd generated she wouldn't be surprised.

She pulled open the door.

"Kai, you should have heard me!" Jordy exclaimed, practically bouncing as he came into the room. "I really nailed that Mayer riff!"

"Did you now?" she said as she stood back to let him past her.

"I played it back, and you can really recognize it!"

"I'll listen to it, if you don't mind."

"Of course not. I want you to, you can tell me—"

He broke off suddenly, and Kai knew he'd spotted his father.

"What are you doing here?"

There was no mistaking the open antipathy in his voice, or the scowl on his face. This could be trickier than she'd thought.

Wyatt didn't speak, just gestured with his coffee mug. Way to answer without lying, she thought.

"Couldn't you just wait downstairs?" Jordy said, teetering on the edge of a resentful whine.

Wyatt again said nothing. Kai wondered how long he'd been putting up with that tone from his son. Judging by his lack of expression, far too long.

"This is my home, Jordy," she said quietly. "I don't care for rudeness."

The boy flushed. "Sorry," he said, but it was to her, not his father. And for the first time she really saw what Wyatt was dealing with on a daily basis. She'd admired him in an abstract sense for taking on the son he'd never known about, appreciated his sense of responsibility, and that he'd literally changed his entire life to take charge of that responsibility.

But now that abstract admiration was becoming something more solid. And she didn't think it was just because he could boil her blood with a touch. Jordy was so different with her that she hadn't quite realized what Wyatt was putting up with one on one, she guessed every day.

"We were just talking about...your father being late to pick you up tomorrow."

Jordy flicked a glance at Wyatt, but then focused on her, as if she were the only one he wanted to listen to.

"How late?"

"Late enough that I'm thinking pizza for dinner."

Jordy brightened instantly. "Really? Up here with you?"

Ouch, she thought at the instant shift from resentment to delight. It was a wonder, Kai thought, that Wyatt didn't hate her for the disparity in the way his son treated them.

"I'm sure your father would like an evening to himself," she said.

"Why? He never does anything. Or lets me do anything."

Again no reaction from Wyatt. Her own father would have taken that tone from her once, and once only.

"Did you ever stop to think that you're the reason he never, as you say, does anything? That maybe he'd be out enjoying himself every night if he didn't feel he had to be a good parent and stay home with you?"

Wyatt moved then, she saw it from the corner of her eye. He set down the coffee mug, staring at her. Jordy merely gaped at her, apparently too stunned to even register the betrayal she was sure he was feeling.

"Don't ruin your relationship defending me," Wyatt said quietly. There was a touch of warning in his voice, and she realized he meant that she wouldn't be able to get what he needed from Jordy if the boy wasn't speaking to her, either.

"You're siding with him?" Jordy yelped, finally finding his voice.

"I'm siding," she said, "with courtesy under my own roof. I can't control outside, but in here, I'll take nothing less. No matter how much I like you."

As she'd intended, her last words calmed him. But he still cast a glare at his father. And Kai couldn't help thinking that she'd landed in an already boiling pot.

Heat of many kinds seemed to be taking over her life just now.

Playing With Fire, indeed.

Chapter 19

"He thinks Max wants a job there, that's why he's asking those questions," Kai said the moment the door to her apartment closed behind them.

Wyatt looked at Kai skeptically. "You believe that?"

"Are you going to blow up at me if I do?"

Considering the way she'd kissed him into near oblivion the moment he'd walked into the store on this sunny Saturday—clearly not worried about anybody walking in—he'd be a fool to do anything of the sort. And after she'd flipped the closed sign over, he wasn't about to.

"No. Just asking."

She gave the question more serious consideration than he would have. She'd spent a few days now trying to glean information from Jordan, after laying the groundwork that night over the pizza. A night which had put Jordan in such a good mood that he was almost civil even to his father for two or three days. A novel experience.

The boy had, she'd told him, seemed to accept that she was just wondering why she hadn't seen Max since he'd come in to pick up his sound gear, and Jordan had offered the theory on his own. He obviously didn't know about Wyatt's confrontation with Max, at least not yet.

"If it was anyone but Max," she said finally, "I would probably believe it. But I know he's up to no good in one area, and after what you told me about that compound in the cold pills... no, I don't believe he's just picking Jordy's brain to try and get a job."

Thank goodness, he thought. She might be overly trusting, but she was far from a fool. And once she realized they were likely dealing with a drug connection, she became as determined as he was.

Kit, he thought, feeling a pang of something as he thought of the years-dead fool. To have had Kai madly in love with him, and then thrown it away was up there so high on the stupid scale he couldn't even give it a number.

"Are you going to call the sheriff?" she asked.

"And tell them what? A suspected drug dealer is talking to my son?"

"Quizzing your son. About a place where they package stuff used in making drugs. They'd at least look into it, wouldn't they?"

"Eventually. In case you hadn't noticed, they're stretched a little thin out here. Literally and figuratively."

"I know. When Mrs. Day had her car stolen, it took them forever to get here because one deputy has to cover the entire north end of the county."

"Besides, there has to be more to this than Max. There's somebody higher up, pulling the strings, and if we spook Max, he'll slip away."

Her brow furrowed as she looked at him. "Why do you think there's somebody higher up?"

"If they're after the product to break it down for the ingredient they need, that's going to be a complicated operation. Max just isn't smart enough on his own."

She was looking at him so intently, those gray eyes troubled, that it blasted all sane thoughts out of his head.

"I can't argue with that," she said. "So what do we do now?"

"You don't want to hear what's first on my list," he said, his voice sounding rusty, rough, even to him.

He hadn't meant to say it. But it was becoming a habit around her, blurting out things he didn't mean to. She didn't even pretend to misunderstand, nor did she take it as a joke and laugh him off. She just looked at him, her eyes widening slightly, as if she felt as completely as he did the sudden heat he'd set off in the room.

"Jordy," she began.

"Will be gone all day on that school trip."

"I know. I was more concerned about what he'll think."

Interesting, he thought, that that was her first thought. And then, belatedly, another realization hit him. Was she actually...considering this?

Molten sensation blasted through him. And in that moment nothing else mattered, not the stupidity of this, or his son's reaction, or what he would likely be doing to himself and the near-peace he'd found here. Not even the idiocy of giving fate another lever to use on him could stand before the fierce, white-hot fever she ignited in him.

"Kai," he said, barely able to find enough air in the room to say her name. Just as well, he thought, because anything else he might say would be to try and persuade her, even push her, because he wanted her more in this moment than he'd ever wanted anything. But it had to be her decision. He couldn't, wouldn't take on the guilt of pushing her into something she didn't really want. His life was a fine balance already, any more guilt would likely tip him over the edge.

And then she looked up at him, those smoky gray eyes suddenly warm and soft. "Let's worry about Jordy later."

He felt a shiver go through him, an odd contrast to the heat leaping along his nerves. "Much later," he said, promise and warning in one.

"Works for me," she said, in a husky tone that hit him much the same way as that same tone did when she sang.

"You're sure?" he asked, feeling he had to even as he told himself he was an idiot.

"Changing your mind?"

"God, no."

He moved before she could change hers. He kissed her, deep and long and for the first time holding nothing back. He didn't know why, it made no sense that this woman, so different from any he'd ever known, would be the one who brought him back to life after so long in the cold. But she had, and no matter his own cautions, no matter the craziness of it, he didn't even want to deny the fact.

His heart was hammering when he finally pulled back. He hesitated one, brief moment, silently giving her one last chance to back away, to change her mind, although he thought it might just kill him if she did.

Instead, her eyes full of a hot sort of wonder that both relieved him and sent even more heat licking along his veins, she reached up to touch first his lips, then her own.

"Wow," she whispered. "That was…as intense as you are."

He sucked in a breath, swallowed tightly. He grasped for the last shreds of sanity left to him. He reached, fumbled in his wallet for the condom someone had planted there as a joking goodbye, the day he'd walked away from his old life. He'd never removed it, thinking it a wry, almost bitter commentary on how badly his life was messed up that it had been there a year, unused, unneeded.

But he needed it now. He'd been irresponsible once, he wasn't going to do it again. Especially with Kai.

"I have exactly one," he said. "I never expected to use it…I didn't expect this, Kai."

"Neither did I," she said, smiling at him in a way that made him feel, for the first time in his life, like the luckiest man on the planet. "Nevertheless, I have a box in the bedroom. Courtesy of my best friend on my birthday a year and a half ago. She hoped I would need them someday soon. It's still sealed."

"Good," he said tightly. "Because one isn't going to be nearly enough."

"Oh, I hope not," she said, in that husky voice that sent ripples of chill and heat through him, ratcheting his already soaring tension up yet again.

He knew he was already out of control by the way his hands fumbled the simple removal of clothing. She helped, and in the growing headiness of heat and need and drive, he wasn't sure who took what off who.

But he was sure he hadn't felt like this in... forever. For a moment, after he kicked free of the last of his own clothes, he just stood there. Never had he literally shook at the sight of a woman's bare curves, shoulders, soft, coral-tipped breasts, and his favorite, that luscious arc from waist to hip.

His gaze snagged on the deep green tattoo, that thin, delicate, intricate circle around her left wrist. He reached out, wrapping his fingers around her wrist over the art. He circled it easily, and it felt delicate yet strong and warm. He liked the mark, he thought. It suited her. Anything bigger or more garish wouldn't have.

She reached out in turn, trailed a single fingertip down from the hollow of his throat to his navel, and he felt like she'd opened him with a hot blade, baring his heart and his very soul to her smokier-than-ever gaze. A shudder he couldn't begin to hide went through him.

That finger veered, over to the scar from a long ago bullet. Her expression changed, just slightly, and he wondered if she was finally having those second thoughts. Maybe she found it repugnant. Maybe he'd accumulated enough scars to make any woman change her mind about wanting a body more battered than they'd expected.

"Someday," she said softly.

He knew what she meant. That someday, she'd want to know the story behind that mark, and probably the others. And she'd want more than "Gun, knife, bomb."

And then she moved that hand lower, laid it

flat against his belly, just above the flesh that surged to meet her touch. And concern about what she might ask, want and deserve from him vanished.

No, wanting wasn't enough of a word for it, not this. Desperate, maybe. Frantic, definitely.

Reckless. Risky.

Yeah, those too.

And none of it mattered. The only thing that mattered was her, and the simply, undeniable fact that if he didn't have her in the next moment there'd be no point in living that long.

"Kai." His voice was a raspy, strained thing he didn't even recognize.

"Are we going to make it to the bedroom?" She sounded like he felt, and this echoing of his own need drove him over the edge.

"Next time," he muttered, handling the condom in the last seconds before he reached for her.

They went down to her plush green sofa in a semi-controlled tumble. He shuddered at the feel of her slender, taut body beneath him. He couldn't get enough, couldn't touch enough. He sucked in a sharp breath when she stroked both hands down his back to cup his backside and pull him closer. And let it out in a long, slow, shivery exhalation as he cupped her breasts and they rounded warmly into his palms.

He ran his thumbs over her nipples, loving that they were already tight and waiting for his touch, shuddering anew at the tiny gasp of pleasure that burst from her.

And then she slid her hand in between them, seeking. He twisted slightly, giving her access he hoped like hell she wanted.

She did. Her fingers curled around him with a sweet, perfect pressure that nearly sent him over the edge right there.

He tried to slow down, tried to rein himself in. And as she so often did, Kai read him perfectly. "There's a time for ballads," she said against his ear, "and there's a time to just let it rip."

She guided him into her slick, welcoming heat. He heard a strangled sound, realized it had come from his own throat. It was difficult at first, and he found that the thought of hurting her had the power he hadn't had himself, the power to slow him down.

"It's been—" her breath caught as he eased a little deeper "—a long time."

He could tell that. "Stop?" he asked from behind gritted teeth; if she said yes, he thought he just might actually die.

She went still. He lifted his head, sensing her gaze on him. "You would, wouldn't you," she said; it wasn't a question.

"There'd be a word for me if I didn't." He ground it out with his jaw still clenched.

She reached up, cupped his face, brought his mouth down to hers. And this time she kissed him, long and deep and impossibly sweet and hot at the same time. In that moment he drove home, smothering her gasp with his mouth, his tongue. And then she was with him, pleasure lacing a deep, heartfelt moan as he began to move. Just the sound of it sent him careening to the edge once more.

And when it became too much, when the caress of her body and the sound of her, the scent of her, the high-strung energy of this vivid free spirit overwhelmed him, he had no choice but to give in and let go.

And she was with him then, too, as her name

broke from him in a rush echoed by his body. She cried out, and in the instant before he lost all awareness, he felt the tight, hot squeeze of her around him.

And he thought that if he did die right now, it would be worth it.

"I like your bedroom."

"What's not to like, at the moment?" she teased. A little to his own surprise, he smiled.

"Not a damn thing. But I do like it." He glanced around at the bold blocks and stripes of color. "It's not frilly."

She laughed. She was snuggled against his side as he lay on his back in satiated exhaustion. What had begun as explosive had, over the course of a long, luscious afternoon, turned into a sweet, slow exploration that had fine-tuned the chemistry between them until the slightest move, the barest whisper set it off all over again.

"Nope," she agreed, "not a frill in sight."

It had been a very, very long time since he'd felt this relaxed. If he ever had. He wished she would have put off the intrusion of reality a little bit longer, but then he glanced at her bed-side clock and realized there was no choice.

"When does Jordy get back?"

So much for relaxed. "In about an hour, if things go as scheduled."

"You're picking him up?"

"At school," he confirmed. "He's supposed to call me if they're early."

"Will he?"

"I doubt it."

She propped herself up on one elbow to look at him, a wry smile curving those soft lips. Odd, he thought. She still seemed so new, so exotic and striking to him, even now. He'd learned every line and curve of her, and she had, to his gasping pleasure, studied every inch of him in a way he'd never known, in a way that made him feel oddly honored, that she thought him worth the effort.

"Are you worried about how he's going to react to this? To us?"

"Do we have to tell him?"

She went very still. "You want to keep it secret?"

That sounded wrong, the way she said it,

like he wanted to hide her away as if he were ashamed.

"Not like that," he said awkwardly. "It's just…he already hates me."

"And you think this will make that worse?"

"I think he'll feel like I'm…trespassing." She considered that, watching him all the while, in a way that made him feel compelled to add, "It's not that I want to hide it, Kai. If it were just me, I'd be yelling it to the world, along with 'eat your heart out.' I wouldn't care who knew." And to his own shock, he realized he meant every word of it.

She smiled then. And reached out to lay her hand on his chest, palm over his heart.

"Good thing we've got an hour, then," she said, her voice soft and husky.

He wondered if she could feel the sudden leap of his pulse, the sudden flush of heat that swept him at her touch. And then she slid her hand downward, over his belly and beyond, and he could barely think at all.

He'd meant it, that he wouldn't care who knew. But it hit him, in the last moments before the firestorm that cascaded through him wiped out all coherent thought, that he should care. That he *had* to care. Because somewhere out there were people who would like nothing better than to know how to get to him.

He'd had no choice about Jordy. But he'd chosen this, chosen her. And it was too late to change that now. Much too late.

It wasn't until he lifted himself over her and she guided him home, and that exquisite, searing sensation of sliding into the hot, slick heart of her swamped him, that he realized he hadn't had any choice about this, either.

Chapter 20

Kai awoke early on Sunday morning. And at first, in those moments suspended between sleep and complete awareness, thought of just going back to sleep simply because she was just so darned comfortable. And then she stretched, and a sudden awareness of certain parts of her body jolted her awake, her breath catching in her throat.

She laid back, closing her eyes, willing the visions of yesterday to play in her head. She'd never known anything like it, not just the fact that they'd spent the entire afternoon in bed, but the succession of changes. The first time had been a flash fire, rising out of nowhere to consume completely. Wyatt had been almost desperate, a feeling she understood perfectly, since she'd been feeling it herself. The second time he'd been gentler, as if he felt he had to make up for his own wildness. The third time had been a long, sweet, savoring kind of thing, that gave her the chance to study him, marvel in what he was doing, and delight in how much pleasure she herself took in simply looking and touching and feeling.

The fact that he had looked and touched in turn, with an expression of awe on his face, hadn't hurt things any. Kai had always assumed the attraction was mutual; Wyatt seemed stunned that it was. She'd thought that one day Jordy's eyes would knock some girl on her backside. She'd never, ever expected his father's to do it to her.

She only realized how widely she was smiling when the muscles of her face reminded her. Pill counter he might be, but Wyatt Blake was one hell of a lover. Who knew? she thought with a tiny laugh.

Now she did. And it had been more than worth closing the store for.

When she finally bestirred herself to get up and head for the shower, she caught a glimpse of herself in the mirror. The only outward signs of what had happened were a red mark on her skin here and there, the fullness of thoroughly kissed lips, and nipples that were tightening at just the memories. She wondered if he, too, wore mementos of their wild afternoon, then felt herself blush as she remembered that she knew he wore at least one; her nails had dug into his back that first time, when they had both gone a little crazy.

"A lot crazy," she admitted to her image in the mirror. "But wow."

If this was what doing without for so long did for you, she'd have to quit thinking of it as, as her friends teasingly called it, a dry spell. From now on, it would be simply building up strength, she thought with a grin at her reflection before she turned and got into the shower, where another encounter had occurred, one that told her without doubt that Wyatt was as strong as she'd thought he might be, from that day with the ax.

Of course, she knew better. She knew that what had happened here had only a little to do with a long stretch of being alone, and much, much more to do with Wyatt. The man was just full of surprises.

She felt a twinge of concern as she finished up and reached for a towel. Wyatt's reluctance had been unmistakable, in fact she'd taken a certain perhaps illaudable feminine pleasure in the fact that he'd wanted her too much to win that fight. Jordy would adapt, she told herself. It might take him a while, but he would. She hoped.

But what she couldn't rationalize away was the feeling that part of Wyatt's reluctance had been for his own sake. To anyone who didn't know the real story, they might assume it was because of his wife's death, but she knew that he had, indeed, barely known Jordy's mother. So what made him hesitate had to be something else, and she didn't know that that something was.

And the fact that you've had sex with him now doesn't give you the right to pry into every corner of his life and psyche, she told herself as she dressed.

Not even if it had been the hottest, sweetest, most life-changing sex ever.

"What's that big building?" Jordan asked.

Wyatt glanced at his son, who was casually— or intentionally—looking out the car's side window and not at him as they headed for his school. It was the first time he'd probed about HP since their first dispute over his sudden interest in his father's job.

"Which one?" he asked, keeping his voice level.

"The green one." He gave Wyatt a quick, sideways look, obviously trying to judge his mood. "Up by the entrance." The boy hesitated, then added in a rush, as if Wyatt had asked for an explanation, "We drove by there in the bus on Saturday, and somebody asked."

Wyatt was fairly certain that had been Max, not someone on the bus. But then, Jordy hadn't exactly said that, had he? He'd worded it ambiguously enough that it was defensible as not being a lie. Not exactly, anyway.

Great. Maybe he was headed for a career as a politician.

Wyatt's mind raced. He'd wrestled with this for the rest of the weekend, time spent keeping Jordan busy when he would have rather been keeping himself—and Kai—very, very busy in that nearly dramatic bed she'd told him was called a sleigh bed. That conjured up images that took his breath away, and memories of her that made him nearly laugh with a kind of joy he'd never experienced. Something she seemed to have the knack for, no small miracle considering how long it had been since he'd laughed about anything.

Even when he'd called her Sunday morning, before Jordan had gotten up, she'd made what he'd been afraid would be awkward joyous instead—he hadn't been sure how you thanked a woman for the most amazing afternoon of your life. But Kai's rich, wonderful laugh and her heartfelt, "It was breathtakingly fantastic, wasn't it? We're magic," made him feel things he couldn't even name.

But the questions he'd been pondering since then were anything but laughable. Because they all involved Jordan, and keeping him out of serious trouble. He could, he knew, open up some channels, talk with some people who knew some other people, and get some action. But he'd sworn to never open that door again. Besides, once one group from his past knew where he was, the word would spread, and until he knew why someone—or several some-ones—had been looking for him already, it wasn't safe.

"The metal building?" he asked Jordan, as if he wasn't answering right away because he wasn't sure what the boy meant, when in fact he was stalling, thinking, wondering.

"Yeah, that one."

If it was anyone else asking, he wouldn't hesitate. The building was, after all, simply the repair shop for that packaging equipment that occasionally broke down.

But this was his son, and he didn't know what to do. He, the man who could always be counted on to have plans A through D going in, and be able to come up with E through G on the fly, couldn't think beyond the fact that his son was headed for trouble. And it seemed like there was nothing he could do about it, short of uprooting them both and moving again.

Which would mean leaving Kai.

The thought of leaving her, at the very time when they'd discovered this amazing thing between them, wrenched at him in a way he'd never felt.

"So what is it?" Jordan asked again.

Control what you can control, be ready to roll with the rest.

The old maxim shot through his mind. Maybe he needed to start thinking of this tactically, and not like a panicked father. If Max thought he'd gotten what he needed from Jordan, maybe he'd drop the boy like a tool he no longer needed. And whatever Max and his cohorts had in mind, it was likely going to happen whether Jordan helped them or not. He couldn't control that.

But maybe he could control what they thought they knew. That building Jordan was asking about was near enough to the main road to be fairly easy to get to from the outside. That made it easy for Max.

But it was also in a cleared area, away from

the offices and other peopled areas, which made it easier and safer to defend.

"It's a storage building, where they keep the incoming shipments so it's out of the way until they're ready to package."

It wasn't perfect, but it was the best he could do on the fly. He doubted Jordan realized he was lying; he might be rusty, but even rusty he was better than most. And the way the boy went rigidly still, as if he were afraid to even breathe, told Wyatt that that answer had been, as he'd thought it might be, exactly what Jordan—meaning Max—had wanted to know.

It felt right, doing something besides holding back and worrying. And that Jordan had probably had to tell Max he was having trouble getting the old man to talk would make it more believable when he finally delivered the goods.

He supposed, had he been a real father, a good one, he wouldn't have done it. But then, if he was a real father, he would have somehow gotten the boy to talk, to tell him the truth. But he'd already long accepted he was lousy at this, so it was time he dealt with it the way the man he'd once been would have. Strategically.

Then again, if he'd done this before, maybe he wouldn't have had to resort to begging for help from the one person his son trusted. And he would have missed out on the most incredible experience of his life.

He again fought down vivid, sizzling images of that afternoon spent in a place he'd never expected to be, feeling things he'd only heard about, wild, huge, crazy things that he hadn't thought himself capable of.

No, running, leaving this place, leaving Kai, wasn't an option he was willing to consider. And all the warnings from that little voice he'd once trusted with his own and other lives couldn't trump that determination.

"I'm sorry, Jordan," he said, almost startling himself; he hadn't intended the words.

Jordan shot him a sideways look rife with suspicion.

"I didn't really realize, before, what it must have been like for you to have to leave everything and everyone you'd ever known."

But now I do, because I know how much I don't want to leave here, leave Kai.

And that scared him. Both the thought of

having to leave, and the thought that it hurt so much. How had that happened, and so fast?

Jordan muttered something unintelligible. Probably just as well, Wyatt thought.

"Someday I hope you'll see I was trying to do the best thing for you."

"Right."

The single bitter word told him Jordan wasn't buying. Not that he'd expected him to, it was just that it had hit him that he'd never really let the boy know that he understood the enormity of what he'd done to him, relative to the teenager's still-limited world.

Later, he thought. He'd have to try again later. Along with all the other things that were being pushed to the rear for the moment. Even the warning emails were filed away. He had to put that nagging concern about possible shadows from his past on hold. He had to trust the assessment that the inquiries had been from friendlies, and thus could likely wait. They had to wait. Just as the questions of why so many and why now—and why they'd stopped—had to wait.

Whoever was looking for him and why didn't

matter at this moment. Because right now Jordan and his safety had to come first. His priorities, he realized, had been permanently changed.

Ironic, he supposed, and typical of the tangled web his life had become, that in order to accomplish that priority, he had to lie, as he had to so many others so many times before.

Jordan would just have to understand, when the time came. Maybe Kai could help with that. Although he wasn't sure exactly where her boundaries were; as much as she hated drugs and what they could do, would she think trying to stop Max would justify lying to his own son? In effect, using the already existing conduit of Jordan to Max to plant false intel? In effect, using Jordan?

He could only hope she would understand. Maybe not agree, but understand.

Right, he thought. *You'll have them both never speaking to you again before this is over.*

The thought clawed at him, leaving bloody furrows he'd swear he should be able to see across his chest over his heart. This is why you don't get involved, he told himself. He'd known that, all along. And he'd managed to live that way, for a very long time.

But that old axiom had never run into the likes of Kai Reynolds.

Chapter 21

"He said he hasn't talked to Max in days. He seemed kind of…hurt about it."

She felt Wyatt, lying beside her with his head cushioned by one upraised arm, go still. He'd been especially fervent this afternoon, hungry, demanding, yet at the same time he still seemed so amazed at what happened between them that it filled her with a wonder of her own. It would have been awful if it had only gone one way. But then, she thought she was right; nothing this incredible could happen if it was only on one side.

"Hurt?" he asked.

"When I was setting him up in the sound

room today, he was awfully quiet. He finally told me Max showed up when he was walking over here from school on Monday. Max said he was busy, and that was the last time they spoke. And Max hasn't been into the store, either."

"Good."

Kai shifted so she could see Wyatt's face. "I guess your warning took."

It surely would have convinced me, she thought. Just one of the many surprises this man was capable of. Not a few of which she'd experienced in the last half hour.

She'd appreciated that he hadn't assumed, when they'd come upstairs after Jordy was settled in the sound room, that they'd immediately leap into bed. Although the idea had a lot of merit, she liked that he left it up to her.

"We only have an hour," he'd said.

"I think we can accomplish a lot in an hour," she'd teased, but had been touched when he'd protested.

"I don't want this to always be some rushed, sneaky thing."

"Never done it on the sly, huh?"

"I have. No more. Not with you."

The simple explanation had moved her in a way she couldn't completely explain. There were depths to this man that weren't just cloaked, they were hidden so deep she wondered if anyone would ever find them. Wondered if he even knew them all himself.

"It wasn't my warning," Wyatt said now. "At least, not completely."

"What do you mean?"

He sucked in a deep breath as he gave her an assessing look. As if he were trying to calculate her response to something.

"Wyatt?"

He sighed. "Max got what he wanted from him."

She blinked. "What do you mean?"

"He got what he was after."

"I thought he was after information on Hunt Packing, on the drugs."

"Yes."

"But Jordy doesn't really know anything...."

Her voice trailed off as it dawned on her just what he meant. And she realized why he'd been wondering about her response to it.

"He pumped you again."

"Yes."

"And this time you answered him."

"Yes."

She supposed she should appreciate that he didn't lie to her, but she was too busy trying to process this. Why on earth would he risk his job, and his apparent friendship with John Hunt, by giving Jordy information that he knew would be passed along to Max? If he was right about Max's intentions, and she thought he probably was, why would he do something that would help that along?

More importantly, why would he risk Jordy getting caught up in the middle of it?

The answer hit her with stark clarity.

He wouldn't.

Everything else aside, the bottom line was simply that he would not risk Jordy.

"You told him so he'd tell Max, who would have no further use for him then. And would leave him alone."

"Yes."

A beautifully simple solution, she thought. Except for one thing.

"But…if you're right about Max and his intentions to steal the stuff from HP, haven't you just helped him?"

"No."

She studied him for a moment, then it came to her.

"You lied," she breathed, staring at him. "You told Jordy exactly what you wanted Max to think."

She thought she saw the faintest trace of a smile begin, perhaps that she had gotten there fairly quickly, before he quashed it and solemnly nodded.

Several things tumbled through her mind in rapid succession. First, relief that she was right, Wyatt would never knowingly endanger his son. Second, that he would also never do harm to someone he felt he owed, like Mr. Hunt.

And third, that for a pill counter, he was awfully darned good at this.

"I thought maybe we could all go get pizza." Wyatt eyed his son's stunned expression. "Unless you're burned out on it."

"Is it possible to burn out on pizza?" Kai asked lightly. "I'd love to. Jordy?"

The boy stared at them, as if sensing the undercurrent between them. Wyatt knew Kai knew this was the beginning. He'd meant what he said, he didn't want to hide this or sneak around. But he also didn't want to slap Jordan in the face with it, and he knew she understood that, too.

There wasn't much her quick mind and sometimes startling perceptiveness missed.

Jordan seemed torn, likely between the pain of being with him, and the lure of being with Kai. The latter, he understood completely.

For that matter, he understood the former, too. And he wondered just how torn the boy would be if he knew that his hated father and his beloved Kai were having rocket-hot sex while he was in that little soundproof room? He'd like to think the boy didn't even know what that meant, but he knew better.

In the end, the lure of more time with Kai—oh, yeah, he understood that—won out, and after she locked up, they walked the three blocks to DiNozzo's. Wyatt said little, just watched and listened as Kai drew Jordan into a conversation about chords and capos and open tuning that was way over his head. But Jordan clearly got it, and he regretted not having realized sooner how passionate the boy was about playing.

They ordered a large pizza, to Kai and Jordan's specifications. He raised a brow at his son.

"I thought you hated mushrooms."

Jordan flushed slightly, since he'd been the one to order them. "I like them on pizza," he said defiantly.

"Just not in spaghetti sauce."

"Yeah." Jordan looked unexpectedly uncomfortable. "I'm gonna go play a game," he said, gesturing toward the small bank of nearly-antique arcade games in the far corner of the dining room.

"What was that all about?" Kai asked.

"A plate of spaghetti he threw at me our third night here."

"With mushrooms, I gather."

Wyatt nodded. Kai gave a slow shake of her head. "He's still very angry at life."

"Funny, I thought it was me he was angry at."

"You're just the convenient target."

Wyatt's mouth quirked. "Been there," he muttered. Then, before she could ask what he meant, he added, "But he's better. Much better, since he's been playing. Thank you for that."

"You're welcome."

"Thank you," he said again, "for…a lot of things."

She smiled, the faintest tinge of color touching her cheeks. "Back at you," she said, her voice taking on that husky note that was like her finger tracing his spine. He had to suppress a shiver as a flood of memories swept over him.

He lowered his gaze to the table, a wooden plank affair most often seen in backyards or parks, for picnics. That would be nice, he thought suddenly, a picnic with Kai.

He nearly laughed aloud at himself even thinking about such a normal thing. But the urge faded; wasn't that why he'd come here, why he'd brought Jordan here, for just that sort of thing, the sort of thing he'd left behind long ago to tread in darkness and too often with evil all around?

He would like that picnic, he thought. A lot. Just as he would like a million other things he never would have thought of, if they were shared with her.

This kind of feeling had never been in his plans when he'd walked away. But then, in the beginning his plans had been simple. Leave it all behind. Go somewhere safe, and tell no one. Try to stay alive.

But as with all plans, the unexpected tended to disrupt them. And in this case, the disruption was indeed unexpected. Unexpected, uncooperative and permanent. He glanced over at Jordan, who was intently blasting something out of existence on an old-fashioned arcade video game.

Probably wishing it was me, he thought glumly.

"He's coming around," Kai said softly. He'd almost gotten used to her reading him so accurately. He who had more than once been told he was the most unreadable man on the planet.

"Maybe," he said, shifting his gaze back to her.

He couldn't quite believe she was there. Or that he was here with her. Something. But she was, and it was far, far too late to backtrack. So now he had to deal with the second major disruption of his plans. Kai and a host of feelings and urges so intense, and so completely new to him that when it came down to it, he had no idea how to deal with them.

"What now?" he asked, not even sure what he meant by the question.

"What do you mean?"

"Never mind," he muttered, wishing he hadn't said it, since he had no idea what he meant.

"Whew," Kai said, in a teasing tone. "For a minute there I thought you wanted to Talk."

He blinked at the way she said the last word. "Talk?"

"You know, with a capital *T.* Usually preceded by a very intense 'We have to.' I hate those."

He laughed, aloud. He couldn't stop himself. "I thought women usually—"

He did manage to stop himself then. And Kai

grinned at him. "A broad generalization nipped in the bud. This is good. You're coming along, too, Mr. Blake."

What I am is crazy, he thought. *Stark, raving, nuts-out-of-the-bag crazy.*

There was a bustle of sound from the doorway, and Wyatt looked up. He was seated with his back to the wall, facing the doorway, a habit he'd never even tried to break. Three young men were there, with a fourth, even younger, standing a few feet away. The fourth left, and the first three sat down at a table outside. Two he recognized vaguely from having seen around town.

The third was Max.

Even through the window he could see that Max was wound up. He was shifting constantly in the chair, one foot bouncing in a quick rhythm. He was tapping his right thumb on the table even faster than the foot was bouncing. None of the three came inside; clearly they weren't here to order pizza.

"Hopefully he'll stay outside," Kai said, and only then did Wyatt realize she'd turned to look at almost the same moment he had.

"Is that what they usually do?"

She nodded, letting out a small, compressed breath. "Yes. He's here almost every afternoon and evening. Most of his customers are thankfully out-of-towners, and I guess they can't find him unless he's out front and visible."

An edge had come into her voice, and he wasn't sure if it was anger or bitterness.

"Then they go around the corner into the alley to complete the transaction?" he asked, remembering what she'd told him.

Kai nodded, and when she looked at him again, her eyes were troubled. "I am sorry, Wyatt. I should have told you right away."

"It's all right." He meant it, he'd long gotten past that.

She shook her head. "I just didn't want to believe it was happening here, in quiet little Deer Creek. That it had…followed me."

He hadn't thought of it quite that way. After a moment he said quietly, "It didn't follow you, Kai. It was already here. You just noticed it because you've been there."

"I should have said something to somebody.

The deputy, he could have investigated Max and stopped him before Jordy—"

She stopped when he held up a hand. "Stopping Max doesn't cure the problem. It's like a weed, unless you get the roots, it's just going to come back."

"You mean…whoever it is that's behind Max?"

He nodded.

She looked at him. "You seem to know a lot about this kind of—"

"I suck at Donkey Kong," Jordy announced, plopping back down at the table. On Kai's side, of course, which Wyatt completely understood. And since he was glad at the interruption, he only smiled at the boy, earning him a grimace.

"I'd be better at it if we had a game system at home. And I could play Guitar Hero. But he barely lets me watch any TV. I don't even have one in my room."

"Not sure you're missing much there," Kai said neutrally. "And third person is very rude, when the person's right here."

It took Jordan a moment to work it out.

Then, to Wyatt's surprise, the boy said, "Yeah. Sorry," in a tone quite unlike the usual grudging insincerity of his forced apologies.

A callout from the counter told them their order was up, and Jordan jumped up without asking and went to retrieve it.

Wyatt couldn't believe this. Couldn't believe he was sitting here, with his son and the woman who had turned his world upside down, doing something as normal as having pizza in a small-town pizza parlor. Only the presence of Max outside was a niggling reminder that all was not blissful, small-town serenity. And for the moment, other than keeping an eye on that table outside, he was willing—no, happy—to ignore that.

Jordan dug into the steaming pizza, and Wyatt himself found it surprisingly good; it had been a while. Kai limited herself to two slices, but she ate those with a relish that made him hot all over again, especially when she unconcernedly licked a drip of sauce from the corner of her mouth. He remembered that mouth on him, kissing, licking, and he nearly groaned aloud at the sudden pressure of a body that hadn't had anywhere near enough of her.

He didn't think he'd ever have enough of her.

They'd finished the pizza, Jordan had gone another few rounds with his game while Wyatt had simply enjoyed being with Kai, talking of simple things that somehow seemed profound to him just now. He felt no desire to put an end to the evening.

It was, however, not the easiest thing for him to sit and watch the occasional customer approach Max. He supposed the upside was that so far there hadn't been anyone he recognized, the downside was that two of them had been Jordan's age, or younger. It went against the grain to just sit there, but he did it.

He heard a distant musical sound and his peripheral vision caught a movement from outside. His gaze shifted in time to see Max taking out what was obviously a smartphone.

Probably needed it to track his business, Wyatt thought, wondering what he'd find if that phone managed to fall into his hands. Perhaps he should facilitate that. There had to be calls to and from his boss there, whoever it was. In fact…

Max's entire demeanor changed as he looked at the phone and saw who was calling. The cocky, local dealer vanished, and an attentive, almost respectful follower appeared.

The boss? Who else could shut Max's smart mouth up and make him simply sit and listen intently?

Maybe Kai, he thought. *She sure worked that kind of magic on Jordan.*

Who, thankfully, was now sitting with his back to the window and was oblivious to Max's presence. Again, most likely thanks to Kai; if it had been just he and Jordan, the boy would be looking any and everywhere except at him, and would have spotted Max long ago. He wasn't sure what would happen, but he didn't want to find out.

He was just thinking of how they were going to get out of here without walking right by Max's improvised sales counter, wondering if there was a back door out of this place, when Max finished the call and put the phone back in his pocket.

Then he leaned forward to talk to his two companions, gesturing them in closer, giving a conspiratorial air to the whole tableau. The two others instantly became alert, glancing at each other with excitement. Max said something to the two, then one of them checked his own cell phone, the other glanced at a heavy, flashy gold watch on his wrist.

Coordinating time, Wyatt realized.

Then they all stood; the local drug connection was apparently closed for the day. Max said something else, there was another checking of the time, then they all nodded and departed to their cars parked near the door; Max to a shiny, near-new German sports sedan, the other two to a Japanese coupe that was much less expensive but covered in flash and bling and with a stereo that could break windows a block away; he'd seen—and heard—it around town.

For a moment after they were gone, he just sat there. But there was no denying what had just happened, and his gut was screaming. He knew too well, had seen it too often to be able to deny it now. The sudden tension, the repeated checking of time, the excitement, the last instructions and the abrupt departure all spelled one thing to him.

Add to it that they'd just gotten a big delivery, in a plainly visible truck, and the sum was clear.

Tonight was the night.

Chapter 22

He had no choice.

He had to get involved in what was going down at HP.

Wyatt sat in the chair again pretending to read while Jordan finished his homework, hearing the refrain in an endless loop in his head.

He had no choice.

Jordan grudgingly but dutifully sat at the table in the den reading a schoolbook. The boy had protested when he'd called an end to the evening out, and it was all he could do not to snap at the boy; it wasn't like he *wanted* it to stop, that idyllic outing with Kai.

"Homework," he'd said.

Jordan had opened his mouth, then glanced at Kai and shut it again. *Probably,* Wyatt thought, *on that word I promised him hell to pay if he used it again.* Although there was no doubt in his mind it had been Kai's presence and not his own threat that had forestalled the boy.

But it hadn't stopped him from trying to enlist Kai's support. "He makes me do my whole weekend's homework on Friday night, can you believe it?"

"Ouch," Kai said empathetically. Then, without even a glance at Wyatt, she'd added, "But at least that means it's done and you don't have to worry about it all weekend."

"Well, yeah," Jordan had admitted grudgingly.

So maybe that was his problem, Wyatt thought now. He'd never explained it to the boy that way, just told him it had to be done because there was other work to do on the weekends.

At first the boy had grumbled every Friday, but gradually the complaints had slowed, whether out of resignation or actually seeing the advantage, Wyatt didn't know. But the whines were seemingly in proportion to the length of the list of chores the boy had for that weekend; if he saw the chance for some real free time, he didn't protest as much.

Wyatt felt a little like protesting himself. But having no choice was not an unfamiliar place for him; he'd been there countless times before, facing something he didn't want to do but had to. And on his own; oh, yeah, that was old, familiar territory.

And this he had to do, for so many reasons. Not the least of which was he owed it to John. The man had paid him back tenfold for whatever he'd done for him, long ago. And if he'd taken the job John had wanted him to take, this would be his baby anyway. But he'd refused, and now the only thing between John and Max and his crew was a twenty-three-year-old rent-a-cop who had never faced anything more dangerous than an errant raccoon. This was way out of his league.

But it was dead-center in Wyatt's.

And to top it off, he'd probably accelerated the timetable, with his confrontation with Max.

He should have thought of that, but the only thing that had been in his mind at the time was keeping the slimy predator away from his son.

The question was, how was he going to do what he had to do when he had Jordan to worry about? What were the chances the rebellious kid would stay put just because he told him to?

Or should he tell him at all? Maybe he should just get Jordan settled in for the night and then leave, do what he had to do. The boy hadn't tried sneaking out again; in fact once he was in his room he always stayed there, reading or listening to music—Relative Fusion, no doubt—probably happy to avoid his father for the rest of the night. He might never know. And he'd be safe enough here in the house; the action was going to be elsewhere.

He was certain Jordan wasn't involved in this portion of it. There would be no reason, and they wouldn't want a kid hanging around to mess up their operation. No, he'd been a source, that was all. Max's abrupt abandonment of the pretense of friendship proved that.

With an effort he kept things seeming normal until Jordan finished and got up to go upstairs, an hour later than usual because it was the start of the weekend. Jordan thought it a ridiculously short concession, and Wyatt wasn't sure he wasn't right, in fact had been thinking about letting the boy have more time, but clearly to-night wasn't the night.

But it might not hurt to put the boy on his best behavior, he thought.

"Jordan."

The boy didn't answer, but he did stop and look back from the foot of the stairs.

"Sometime this weekend, let's talk."

The boy's expression became wary, and Wyatt had a sudden image of Kai—like that was unusual, he thought wryly—saying *Whew, for a minute there I thought you wanted to Talk.*

He smiled in spite of himself, and Jordan's expression shifted from wary to puzzled. Wyatt sighed inwardly; maybe he really should lighten up on the kid.

"About you maybe staying up a little later on Friday and Saturday."

Jordan blinked. "Really?"

Wyatt nodded. "If you behave and we can work out an agreement on the terms."

The boy grimaced, but Wyatt had a feeling it was more about the businesslike wording than anything. Jordan gave him a quick nod, and an expression that was as close to a smile as he'd gotten from the boy since this chaos had begun.

He wondered if that smile would get wider or vanish when he found out about his father and his beloved Kai. Wyatt had no idea. And he didn't have time to think about it now, he had other things he had to focus on.

He found himself pacing as he thought. If it were him, he'd wait until the deadest hour of the night, but these guys were amateurs. They might jump the gun, just wait until the last of the late shift employees left, which would be in about another hour.

He had to be at HP by then. Before Max and his crew got there, so his arrival wouldn't draw their attention.

He walked into the living room and stood at the foot of the stairs. He just stood there for a long, silent moment, knowing he was on the brink of doing something he'd sworn he was done with.

He had no choice.

Once it had been easy, turning off everything but the focus on the job. Now it was hard. So hard he wondered if he was going to be able to do it.

He had no choice.

So if you can't do it, at least act like you can.

He went to the drawer in the kitchen where the usual household tools accumulated. He took out both a Phillips and a flat-bladed screwdriver. He walked back to the stairs.

The urge was there, to stand and stare again, but it would accomplish nothing. It wouldn't change what he had to do, no miracle answer would appear.

He didn't want to do this.

He had no choice.

He crouched down and went to work with the Phillips, unscrewing the brass crossbar that held the stairway carpet runner snug against the base of the riser of the first, the widest step. He set the bar aside, then used the flat blade to pry the carpet loose from the tack strip at the bottom. Then it was back to the Phillips to undo the wood screws that held the tread of the bottom step in place.

In moments he had removed the tread and was staring down into the storage locker he'd built there. He remembered the day he had sealed it up, the time he'd spent arguing with himself, telling himself that if he was really walking away he'd get rid of it all.

But he'd known even then he couldn't do that. He'd made some very nasty people very angry over the years, the kind of people who would come after him in an instant, if they could find him. And he knew those same people wouldn't hesitate to take their anger out on an innocent boy, if he was connected to him.

He gave himself a fierce mental shake. *You know what the motions are, go through them,* he ordered silently.

He took out the long protective storage pack that held the Mossberg pump shotgun, since it was the biggest and took up the most room and blocked everything else. It had been untouched since he'd cleaned, prepped and sealed it into the protective storage bag. He set it on the floor beside him. He took out the canvas pack that held in various pockets cable ties suitable for use as flex-cuffs, a pair of wire cutters, a single strand flexible saw blade, a small bag that in turn held a powerful monocular, a K-bar style knife and a couple of grenades. He kept the monocular, flex-cuffs and one of the grenades; not the lethal one, but the stun grenade commonly known as a flash-bang.

In the right side of the locker was a sealed storage can holding nine boxes of .45 caliber ammunition. He took that out and set it aside as well, leaving in place the similar can of shotgun shells.

Two smaller sealed storage packs came next. He chose the larger of the two, and used the flat-bladed screwdriver to tear it open. He undid the brown gun wrap, revealing the weapon that had saved his life more times than he could count. The compact .45 HK USP looked as pristine as the day he'd put it into storage, with the promise to himself that in ten years, if he hadn't had to come for it, he would then empty the cache and take his chances.

And here he was, barely a year later, doing

what he'd never wanted to do again. And telling himself all the reasons he should do nothing more than keep Jordan safe didn't change a thing. He wondered if there was something in his DNA, buried deep, that made him as incapable now as before to just walk away.

He had no time for useless questioning, he reminded himself. He started to move quickly then, as if speed of motion could overcome the reluctance. He put the shotgun bag back in the step-locker. He stripped down the HK, wiping parts as he went, although he'd taken such care in packing it up it wasn't really necessary. He did it anyway; he hadn't survived without taking every possible precaution.

He was slower than he used to be putting the weapon back together, this time putting back the spring that he'd kept separate to avoid it losing any strength from long storage. He'd lost a step there, and he'd better remember that he'd likely lost a step elsewhere, too.

He slid the HK's magazine out of the bag, and the spare. Then he opened the ammo can, took out the first box, and loaded the first magazine.

Then began the second; if he needed more than that, he was probably going to die anyway.

At the thought he hesitated, then opened the second bag, taking out the small, two-inch .38 revolver. He dug down until he found that ammo, loaded it, then pulled out the black nylon ankle holster from the bottom of the locker. He strapped it on and slipped the little five-shot inside. Insurance, he thought. He had to think about that now.

That done, he turned back to the HK. He finished loading the backup magazine, his fingers remembering automatically what his mind had tried so hard to forget.

He put the magazine he'd just filled in his back pocket. He picked up the first one, aligned it with the slot in the grip. For a moment he just crouched there, staring at the tools he'd put away with such care, because it was so ingrained in him. Resistance was still growling inside him.

"No choice." He said it aloud this time, as if that would finally pound it into his head.

He slammed the magazine home, and the

sound of it was like a trigger, and he felt the old, cool determination start to well up in him.

A small sound came from above. He froze. Looked. The familiar weapon tracked the change, like an extension of his vision.

His son was staring down at him from the top of the stairs, eyes wide with shock.

Chapter 23

Trying to solve the enigma that was Wyatt Blake was exhausting, Kai thought. That he'd wanted them to go out, all three of them, was touching. Although he hadn't said anything to Jordy to indicate this was anything more than just grabbing a meal together because they happened to be together, it still seemed significant to her. Proof he'd meant what he'd said, that he didn't want to keep it—them—a secret.

And he'd seemed to enjoy the evening, even with Max conducting his slimy business just outside the door. And that was on her list of things to do tomorrow; maybe Wyatt didn't think there was enough proof, but she was going to call somebody anyway. She wanted there to be a record that someone had reported it, even if it took them forever to get to it.

All through dinner, and after, when they'd just been chatting, Jordy even joining in a little, Wyatt had been watching Max. And then he'd gone...not cold, but distant somehow, as if his mind were completely elsewhere, and he'd ended things rather abruptly. She thought it might have something to do with the way Max and his buddies had also left rather abruptly, but Wyatt had said nothing about it. And Jordan's homework was a legitimate excuse, but she couldn't help thinking that was exactly what it was, an excuse.

And something about Wyatt nagged at her. He hadn't just changed in his demeanor, he'd changed in a deeper way, right before he'd ended the evening. It was almost visible to her, a sudden steely determination and cool detachment. This wasn't the man struggling with a teenage son, or even the passionate lover who had so startled her. This was the suspicious, edgy man she'd first met in her store that day, only much, much worse. There had been something almost frightening about him, in those last few minutes, although Jordy had seemed unaware. But she was aware, she felt it coming off him in waves.

She told herself to give it up, she had no answers so it was useless to keep pacing her living room wondering. She thought of going down to play, but for one of the few times in her life the idea held little appeal. She should do that paperwork she'd been putting off, or update her banking data, count strings, something.

Or just go to bed, she thought. It was nearly ten anyway. Early for her, but late enough for most, she thought.

Sure, she muttered inwardly. *You can lie there awake for a couple of hours, trying to figure out the man while you toss and turn wishing he was here.*

Because, she realized with a little shock, she wanted to sleep with him. Literally. She wanted to feel his warmth in the night, and more urgently, wake up with him in the morning.

A little shiver went through her at the thought. She shook her head sharply, warning herself she was falling too far, far too fast. For all the good it would do. She might not be able to figure Wyatt out, but what she did know— that he was an edgy, sometimes harsh man that half the time she suspected wasn't at all what he appeared to be—should be enough to convince her to tread carefully. And yet here she was....

Her cell phone rang, a welcome distraction tonight. Wyatt? she wondered as she ran to the kitchen counter where she'd set her purse. He'd called her several times before, in the evenings after Jordy had gone to bed, once she'd told him she was nearly always up until midnight. She'd found the calls sweet and a little awkward, because he'd sounded like he didn't even know why he was doing it, when they'd just been together a few hours before.

And that was a thought that made her smile as she pulled the phone out and glanced at the screen. Not Wyatt. This was the call she'd been waiting for for days now. And for a moment she pondered whether she really wanted to answer, if she really wanted to know....

With a sigh, she clicked on.

"Hey, girl!"

David King's cheerful greeting echoed in her ear.

"Hey, Davy. How are you?"

"About the same as when you called before," David said, and she could see her old friend and bandmate's irrepressible grin as clearly as if he were standing there, twirling a drumstick madly with his fingers as if it were a propeller.

"A little nuts, you mean?"

"I'm a drummer at heart, y'know? Comes with the territory."

They shared the laugh about old times, and then he turned to business. Which in this case, revolved around his other skill; David's nimbleness with drumsticks was more than matched by his nimbleness with a computer keyboard. He'd run the band's internet presence with skill and knowledge, taking Kai's ideas and running with them. He had once considered hacking a hobby. He'd thankfully retired that for the most part.

Except when it was a favor for a friend.

"So, what's your interest in this guy?"

Uh-oh. David hadn't asked that before, as

she knew he wouldn't; he was a no-questions-asked kind of friend if you needed help. That he was asking now told her he'd found something that made him, at the least, curious, at the most, protective.

"He's the father of a kid who comes in here every afternoon to practice."

"Okay, that tells me who he is to you, but not what."

David, for all the jokes in the music world about drummers, was far from stupid.

"You tangled up with this guy?" he asked.

An image shot through her mind, of herself, quite literally—and nakedly—tangled up with Wyatt just hours ago. He'd learned her so quickly, found every sensitive, nerve-loaded spot on her body, and then proceeded to play them better than she played BeeGee. And she'd tried to learn him in turn, returning the favor. And she'd succeeded, except for the scars he bore and his reluctance to talk about them, insisting they were the result of simple accidents. He'd distracted her—intentionally?—by asking if they bothered her, with just enough uncertainty to trigger a protective urge in her. She'd proceed to make those scars a starting point for caressing him, kissing him, until she was sure he knew that nothing could detract from how beautiful she found him.

Because she did find him beautiful, lean, strong and with that subtle grace that sent frissons of heat through her every time he moved.

But the nature of those scars, especially the one she had finally realized was from a gunshot, had always run a tiny thread of unease through the joyous passion that was so utterly new and precious to her.

And now she was very much afraid she was about to find out that unease was well-founded. She drew in a breath to steady herself, then said it.

"How bad is it?"

"Bad?"

"Is he on the run?" It was one of the many ideas that occurred to her when she pondered the mysterious Mr. Blake and his scars.

"Maybe," David said. "But probably not the way you mean."

She blinked. "What is he, a protected witness or something?"

"Closer," he said. "You really don't know?"

"Obviously," she said, trying to keep annoyance out of her voice; David did like to play people a bit.

"He's not a protected witness, but he's put a few people there."

She frowned. "What? Come on, David, don't play with me."

He relented. "He was a fed."

She blinked. "What?" she repeated, stunned. A fed? A federal agent? FBI or CIA or something?

"And he's something else, Kai."

Something had come into David's voice that made her shiver inside. "What?" she asked weakly for the third time.

"He's a freakin' hero."

Chapter 24

She'd been right all along, Kai thought. Wyatt Blake was not what he seemed.

She sank down into the big, overstuffed chair that took up the space by her front window.

"Give it to me," she ordered David.

"You want the whole list?"

"Yes."

She could almost see the stocky drummer shrug. "Joined the FBI right out of college—"

"Where?"

"College? UCLA. Cum laude. Big time. Bet they recruited him."

"Yes." She wasn't surprised. She'd known he wasn't stupid.

"According to what I found, took the usual path, heavy training, tactics, weapons, all that. Moved around a bit the first couple of years. But he racked up some awards, commendations and stuff, bank robberies and the like. He was given his own field office fairly early, although I guess it was a small one, only two agents."

"Where?"

"Montana. Lot of territory there. Anyway, they foiled what would have been a nasty terrorist plot, stopped a truckload of explosives and weapons smuggled in over the border. Lots of news articles about that one. The bad guys had built a false floor in a livestock truck, then put real sheep in it. Clever."

She grimaced. "Scary."

"Yeah, that too." He chuckled. "Your boy was a hero, they decorated him like a Christmas tree, but he got in a little trouble too. Turns out he told the bad guys the truck had originally transported pigs. Didn't go over well."

Kai nearly laughed aloud at that.

"Anyway, he apparently got a say in where he went from there. Transferred to the L.A. office, saved a couple of kidnap victims, took down some seriously armed bank robbers, piled up a ton more awards and medals, or whatever they give those guys. Then he went under."

"Under?"

"Only thing I could find was that he ended up on a crack special assignment team. A supersecret special assignment team. I don't think he was still FBI at that point. Maybe not even CIA. This stuff is way, way under."

Kai fought to absorb it all. She felt nearly dizzy with all the revelations, and had to force herself to focus.

"He really was a hero," she said, shaking her head in shock.

"Several times over, from what I found."

"But…why did he leave?" Her breath caught. "He *did* leave? You did say he *was* a fed."

"Yeah. I found a record of his resignation from federal service as of about a year ago."

"Was it…because he'd been shot?"

"Shot? Don't know about that. No record of that, so it must have happened after he went into that supersecret unit. How'd you know?"

"I've seen the scar."

There was a moment's pause, and she could imagine what David was thinking, what he was guessing. But for once, he didn't tease her. Maybe something was sounding in her voice that warned him off.

"I don't know why he quit," he said briskly. "He'd been at it for almost seventeen years. Maybe he just burned out. I'd think that kind of work would do it to you."

"Yes. Yes, it would." No wonder he assumed most people lied. In his work, the ones he dealt with probably had.

"I could keep digging, if you want, but those walls are high and thick. Not sure I could get much further without crossing some dangerous lines."

"No, David. You've done enough, don't get yourself in trouble over this."

"Thanks," he said, sounding relieved.

"One more thing, though," she asked as a cogent thought finally worked its way through her daze. She hesitated. She wasn't a snoop by nature, figuring that most people would eventually tell her what they wanted her to know.

But she wasn't in love with most people.

She smothered a gasp as her mind formed the words for the first time. David's words cut off her thoughts, and she'd never been more grateful for an interruption.

"Sure, Red, what?"

She shoved the stunning revelation aside for the moment and calculated quickly back from Jordy's birthday, which he'd glumly told her was right after he'd moved here, and that it had sucked.

"Where was he fourteen years and three months ago?"

David didn't comment on her specificity. "Let's see, I've got it all here…he was in L.A. by then, but barely. And he was there for a couple of years before the uber-secret stuff started. So that would cover your fourteen and three."

So it fit, she thought, that that was where Jordan was conceived. And born. And had lived until tragedy struck and he found himself out in the woods of the great Northwest.

"Any more details on what he did in L.A.?" she asked.

"Looking," David said, as if he were scanning data, as she supposed he was. "Yeah. He was there barely long enough to unpack before he landed a kidnapping that got him yet another decoration. Bet that's what got him the attention of this other unit, because he went in undercover, news article says, saved a woman and got back the ransom, practically single-handedly."

"A woman?"

"Yeah. Some rich guy's daughter. Got snatched right out of her college dorm."

Jordy's mother? Had he gotten involved with a victim? Wasn't that verboten?

"Hmm," David said. "Twins."

"What?"

"The woman had a twin sister. Sounds like she was a big help in the case. She was all 'my hero,' but your boy said they couldn't have done it without her."

Your boy. She tried to get a grip on emotions that were piling up behind the dam she'd hastily thrown up. She fought for calm, for logic.

"Can you find anything about the sisters? What happened to them after?"

"Probably. Hang on."

Kai waited, heard the faint sound of keyboard keys clicking, then a pause, then more clicking. She focused on the sounds intently, making herself try to imagine what he was keying in, postponing the moment when she was going to have to start processing all this.

"Michelle Price, the kidnapped sister, moved to Europe. Wanted to leave it all behind, I guess. Oh, wow, that's sad," David said.

"What?"

"Melissa, the other sister, died a few months ago. There's an obit online. Cancer. Sucks."

Melissa. Jordy's mother. She had her answers.

"Thanks, David."

"You okay?"

"I'm not sure."

"You having a problem with this guy? Want me to come kick his ass?"

She thought it much more likely it would go the other way around, but she didn't say so.

"Not that kind of problem, but thanks for

the offer," she said. "He's just been…less than forthcoming about who he is. Or was."

"Maybe he's got reason," David said. "Sounds like he could have some nasty memories piled up."

"Yes," she agreed, thinking of the first time she'd seen him, of the exhaustion she'd noticed even then, dulling the eyes that were so vividly green in his son.

Pill counter indeed, she thought. But she was beginning to see, perhaps, why he'd gone for such a mind-numbing job. Maybe he'd wanted exactly that, his mind numbed into forgetting.

She thanked David again, and after reassuring him once more that she was all right, she hung up. And for a long time simply sat there, a little numbed herself. She couldn't believe this. She, the one-time rebel, had fallen—and fallen hard—for an ex-fed.

There was a time when, flush with youthful rebellion, she might have been angry that he'd been a cop. But she'd outgrown that some time ago, and what she valued had grown up as well.

He's a freakin' hero….

David's words echoed in her head. A hero. No denying that.

She could even picture it, how Jordy had happened. The long hours of tension about her missing sister, the relief, the promises of no recriminations, no strings. She could believe it now that she had the last missing piece.

She jumped to her feet, unable to sit still any longer. At last the anger had broken through. Not at what he had been, but that he had kept it so hidden. Not just from her, although that was perhaps the worst. She had the right to know exactly who she had handed her heart over to, didn't she? Who she was having body-blasting, life-altering sex with?

She was barely aware of pacing the room. Or gradually going faster. Her thoughts were still racing far ahead of her actions.

It wasn't just her, he hadn't told anyone. He'd let all of Deer Creek think he had just vanished out there after college, doing nothing of note. Certainly not being a hero.

He hadn't told his own son.

He used to be a paper pusher and now he's a pill counter...how lame is that?

Boring.

Maybe he had his reasons for keeping his heroic past a secret. But couldn't he at least have had the decency to acknowledge he was doing it? A simple "It's there, but I don't want to talk about it," would have done. Maybe "I have a past but I haven't done anything criminal or immoral." Maybe even just, "I was one of the good guys, Kai." That would have been nice. Didn't she have the right to know at least that much?

She was building up a good head of steam now, and was about at the end of that fuse she'd worked so hard to lengthen over the years. Maybe she was more upset than she realized about...not being lied to, at least not directly, but not knowing who she'd fallen in love with.

Because she most definitely had fallen.

And she wanted some answers.

She quickly changed into heavier shoes, and grabbed up her jacket and a scarf; the days were still end-of-summer warm, but the nights held the scent and coolness of encroaching fall.

She belted down the stairs. Glanced at her car, sitting and dutifully waiting.

No, you should walk, she told herself. Get a grip on your temper. Burn some of it off before you jump down his throat.

And figure out how you're going to explain that you went snooping into a part of his life he obviously wanted kept secret. Yeah, that was a problem.

He was just going to have to understand. And if he didn't, or couldn't, or wouldn't, well, better she know it now, before she got in any deeper.

Yeah, right....

Even to herself the sarcasm was sizzling.

It didn't take her long to cover the few short blocks. The main street still had some activity on this Friday night, but the residential streets were quiet and calm, as befit the near-rural little town. There were no streetlights out here, but with the almost full moon it was hardly necessary; the lighting was stark and silver, but she could probably read by it if she had to.

Her steps slowed as she got close enough to see the house. The house was dark except for one faint light in an upstairs window. Had he already gone to bed?

Tough, she thought; the walk had taken the edge off her anger, but only just.

She sped up again. She would confront him anyway. Wake him up if she had to. Make him talk to her. You just didn't keep that kind of secret from somebody you were intimate with.

Unless, of course, you didn't feel the same way.

Her steps slowed once more as she reached the foot of the long driveway. Maybe that was it. He hadn't told her because he wasn't all that emotionally involved with her. Maybe it was just all hot sex for him. He'd never said anything to indicate it was anything more. She was the one who had—

A movement caught her eye, somewhere near that lit window. She narrowed her gaze, trying to see in the moonlight that exaggerated the shadows. She changed course and walked up the driveway; the walkway veered away from that side of the house, the side where Wyatt had been chopping wood that day.

Heat flooded her, warding off the night's growing chill easily. She'd thought he was fit and lean and taut that day.

Now she knew exactly how right she'd been, inch by glorious inch.

Stop it, she ordered herself. *You're not going to get this done if you can't stop salivating over the guy.*

And then she stopped dead, finally able to see what had caught her eye.

Jordy. Dropping from the big tree beside the house to the ground, obviously having climbed out his bedroom window. She nearly called out, then stopped herself; she was far enough away that if she made enough noise to catch his attention, she'd end up waking the whole neighborhood. She doubted Wyatt would appreciate that.

She hurried up the long driveway. Saw Jordy dart into the garage through a small side door. He came out wheeling a bike she'd seen before. He never even glanced her way, even though by now she was barely twenty feet away. He jumped on the bike and took off, not as she'd half expected, toward town, but to the west into the woods behind the house, the small red light on the rear of the bike glowing.

She did call out then, but Jordy either didn't hear or ignored her. He'd left that side door open, and she instinctively went to close it. And stopped.

This made no sense. He never, ever left Jordy home alone. But there was no denying the simple, obvious fact that the garage was gapingly empty. No black SUV was parked inside.

She glanced back at the house. Up at where the light still gleamed in the window.

The broken window.

She took a step closer, but there was no doubt that the bottom half of the window glass was broken; the edge of a blue curtain was fluttering through to the outside.

She looked toward the woods, where Jordy's red light was growing fainter. Go, she thought. Doing nothing was not an option; for her it never had been. Not even now, as angry and confused as she was.

She had to do something. Because she

couldn't deny one simple fact, whether it made sense or not.

Wyatt was gone, and Jordy was alone.

Chapter 25

Amateurs, Wyatt thought.

Definite amateurs. And that bothered him. If an illegal drug manufacturer had survived to the extent that he felt capable of both expanding to larger quantities and going after the ingredients to do it, he would have expected a little more polish. But then, he would have expected them to have their own talent, and not hire local. Especially not clearly inexperienced local kids like Max and crew.

He admitted his specialty had never been drug enforcement, but he'd come across enough of it, since it was frequently used to finance other types of operations. And this just didn't feel right.

He braced his left arm on the large limb of the tree—nearly a twin to the one next to the house—and leaned forward with the small monocular lens in his right hand. Even without the night vision capability, the moon was so bright he'd figured it could help. He'd picked out this spreading tree days ago, when he'd first realized what Max was planning. When skulking around where they shouldn't be, especially outside, people tended to look around, behind, over their shoulder and ahead, but rarely up.

Unless they were pros, which Max and his buddies certainly were not. They'd arrived in an unmarked bobtail truck painted a bright white that gleamed in the moonlight, about as concealable as a neon sign, and instead of parking some stealthy distance away as he had, they'd driven all the way to the edge of the HP property.

They'd tried to pull it off the road and into the trees, but the box of the truck was too tall to go very far that way, and there was some significant noise as branches scraped along the top and sides. Plus, they nosed it in, so that the more difficult backing out would have to be done if they were discovered.

Wyatt had already been here and in position when they'd arrived. He'd been used to much longer, often uncomfortable hours of patient waiting. Being in a rush had killed more agents than anything else but poor planning or being just plain stupid.

And he tried not to dwell on the fact that too many times, smart agents got stupid when emotions were involved. And Jordan was in this, even if only on the fringes.

At least, he hoped it was only the fringes.

Wyatt knew he was going to have a hell of a lot of explaining to do when he got home. Talk about stupid, he should have realized when he'd seen the boy's music player on the desk in the den that he'd be coming back down for it once he realized he'd forgotten it. He seemed to live half the time with earphones on, blocking out the world.

More likely blocking you out, he told himself sourly.

His mouth tightened. Locking Jordan in his room, even locking the window with a warning that if he tried to leave he would regret it for the rest of his possibly shortened life probably hadn't been the best approach, but he didn't know what else to do. The thought that what he'd done was worthy of his own father's approach was something he was trying not to think about.

Just as he was trying not to think about that stunned look on his son's face as he had silently watched his father dig out the past he'd hoped never to see again.

Yes, a lot of explaining. And not just to his son. If he'd told Kai the truth, he could have left Jordy with her. But it was all too much to explain when seconds were critical.

It was not something he was looking forward to. He'd wanted to put that life behind him and keep it there. He wished he could do the same with the memories, wished he could regain the trust and faith in his fellow man that let most people function in a much more pleasant world.

Like Kai.

Maybe I just don't want to live my life assuming everyone's guilty until proven innocent.

Yes, just like Kai.

He fought down the ache that rose in him. He didn't want to think about how this might affect her, affect them, either. Would she be angry, stunned, or repelled by who he really was? He had little doubt that she'd be all of those if she knew some of the things he'd done, and no amount of telling himself it had been necessary, and even believing it, could assuage the fear that he was going to lose them both, before he'd ever really had either of them.

Later, he muttered to himself, and shoved the confrontation that was sure to come into its own compartment until this was over.

He waited. If it had been him, he would have gone in through the roof vents, secured only with a pressure latch. But he was guessing these guys would go for the side door that faced away from the main packaging building.

That seemed to be their intent when, wearing ski masks, they carried a large pair of wire cutters to the fence that surrounded the HP property. They argued—loud enough to be heard by anyone within fifty feet—over who was going to make the cuts. In the stark, high-contrast moonlight, it was a bit like watching a very old

black-and-white cartoon, and in the old days
Wyatt might have been grinning to himself.

Now he just wanted this over.

They cut a path through the chain-link fence.
Instead of doing it low and harder to notice,
they simply cut a big gap, obviously not caring
if it was found.

They went through the fence relatively
quietly. This is where it got tricky, because
they were now in the very dark shadow of the
metal building, and in their dark clothes and
ski masks—they'd thought of that, at least—
they were for all intents and purposes invisible.

Wyatt dropped from the tree, landing with
the faintest of thuds in the spot he'd already
cleared of betraying leaves and sticks. In a
crouch he moved quickly to his pre-chosen
spot, just above the fence and behind a large
juniper bush. He heard one of them say something, but they had apparently realized their
error and were whispering now.

He heard movement, and it seemed to him
that it was farther away, but now was the
time he really missed the night vision capac-
ity; he couldn't see a thing. But then he heard

the sound of metal on metal, a push-pull kind of sound, and he guessed they were trying to poke a hole in the metal of the building. He focused on that sound as he reached into his jacket pocket and pulled out the small cylinder he'd taken from the locker.

The sound changed then; he heard them start on the door, apparently using the hole they'd made to insert the same wire cutters to cut through the metal sheeting around the door lock. Not a bad idea, if you had unlimited time. Which apparently they thought they had.

He gave them enough time to get thoroughly focused on the job. Then he moved, edging forward until he was within range of an easy toss. He lobbed the flash-bang.

The stun grenade landed neatly between the two working on the door. Wyatt turned away and covered his ears to avoid the blinding flash of light and the explosive, ear-splitting sound. A split second later he was moving, drawing the HK as he went. The man with the wire cutters was howling, rolling around on the ground with his hands over his ears. His partner had staggered back against the metal wall of the building, completely disoriented.

Wyatt had them rounded up and flex-cuffed before they fully recovered from the shock. He swiftly fastened them with more plastic ties to an intact pole of the fence, his mind screaming all the while; the third man had vanished. That was the movement he'd heard, after the whispering.

He yanked the ski masks off the two he'd caught.

Max. Max was the missing man.

He swore under his breath. "Where is he?"

Neither man answered.

"I don't have time to play nice with you two," he said, leveling the HK at the one who looked like he was recovering faster from the shock of the stun grenade. "Where's Max?"

The man looked so shaken Wyatt wasn't sure he was even comprehending. He jammed the barrel of the HK up under his chin, digging it in deep, until the man gagged.

"He…saw something move," the man choked out. "Over in the trees."

The man jerked his head toward the thick stand of cedars at the far corner of the building.

"Is he armed?"

"He's always got his knife."

Well, he may have a knife, but it wasn't *his* knife, because I've got that, Wyatt thought. He pulled back the HK, slid it into the holster at the small of his back, and took off in a low, crouching run in the direction the man had indicated. He wanted this wrapped up tonight, and until Max was where he should be, this wasn't over.

The shadows in the grove of cedars were different, in some places just as dark as beside the building, but some places lighter where moonlight shone through. All his newly reawakened instincts were screaming, and the skin at the back of his neck was tingling in the old way that used to warn him someone was watching. The motion of the branches in the slight breeze made it even more difficult, and he slowed to move carefully.

"Stop right there, asshole."

From his left, Max's voice. Laced with a confident, even arrogant tone that said he knew he had the upper hand.

Wyatt spun around, weapon raised into plain sight. If Max indeed had only a knife, best he knew he was literally outgunned from the get-go.

And then relative armament, and everything else, became a moot point. Because even in the oddly dappled shadows Wyatt couldn't deny the grim truth of what he saw.

It was Max, all right.

He indeed had a knife.

And it was pressed to Jordan's throat.

Chapter 26

Jordan had been struggling, so strongly that Wyatt's throat tightened; Max wasn't that good and he didn't want him slicing the boy by accident. But he wasn't sure his son would listen if he told him to stay calm. Hell, he wasn't sure if he'd listen if he told him to breathe.

He kept his weapon rock-steady and high; Max was a half a foot taller than Jordan, so there was plenty of clear target.

But there was also that knife, a near duplicate of the one he'd taken from him. He guessed Max didn't want anyone to know about that. Or maybe he lost them all the time and bought them by the dozen. He should have been doing research on the guy, he thought in disgust. He should have been assessing the enemy, but instead he'd been…

His mind, which had been racing at light speed, threatened to seize up at the memories of how he'd been spending his afternoons.

"I should have known you'd try to mess things up," Max said. "I knew you were gonna be trouble."

With a tremendous effort Wyatt made himself shove it all aside, everything but the moment and keeping Jordan safe.

"Since I told you what would happen if you came near my son again? You should have believed me."

Wyatt had been told, more than once, that he could stare down a charging bull. He'd thought the joke hyperbole, but he did know he could have a certain effect when he wanted to.

He wanted to now. Desperately.

It took a greater effort than it ever had to summon up that focus, that intensity. Especially since the back of his neck was tingling in warning that there was something he was missing.

"You have one chance," he said, barely aware

that his voice had dropped to a low, lethal-sounding rumble. "Let him go and leave here alive."

He heard a tiny gasp. He knew it had come from his son, but he didn't shift his gaze from Max's face, his eyes. He was aware that Jordan had stopped struggling. With his peripheral vision he could see that the boy was staring at him.

Max blinked. Instinctively drew back a half-step. Wyatt closed in. For the moment he had to ignore that lingering sensation, hoping it was just a misfire after lack of use.

"You're a cop, aren't you? Asshole Hunt brought in a narc, undercover."

"I'm not a cop anymore. Worse for you."

Max blinked. "What?"

"I don't have to follow their rules."

Again Jordan gasped, but he kept his gaze on Max, who tightened his grip on Jordan.

"You can't shoot me," he said. "I'll cut his throat."

Wyatt shrugged. "Your muscles might try to move after the bullet scrambles your brain.

He might need some stitches. You'll need a coffin."

Max's fingers trembled. He immediately tightened them around the handle of the knife, but Wyatt knew he'd seen the betraying motion.

"But you won't get a coffin. Because nobody will ever find you. You'll just…vanish."

Max was sweating now, despite the cool air.

"Toss the knife here and step back, Max. Now. Last chance."

There was a silent split second when Max hovered between pride and death.

He tossed the knife. As it landed halfway between them, he let go of Jordan.

Wyatt breathed again, but didn't relax. The boy didn't move, just stood there, staring, his eyes wide with shock.

Wyatt took a step toward his son.

"I don't think so."

The voice came from the trees, and Wyatt whipped around. The dappled shadows masked everything. And then a more solid shadow separated from the rest, and stepped out into the moonlight.

For an instant it was like a situational target

range, where a silhouette target popped up and you had to assess in a split second whether it was a danger—mother with baby or suicide bomber with explosives?—and whether to fire.

He would have shot this one, instantly. Because there was no mistaking, even in the dark, the lethality of the Beretta in his hand.

Wyatt's finger tightened on the trigger. He didn't, couldn't fire. Because there was no mistaking where the pistol was aimed.

Jordan.

And there was no way the man, who looked vaguely familiar, could miss the boy at this range.

It was a standoff.

"I knew you were there," Max sputtered at the newcomer. "I knew you'd have a gun on him, so I—"

"Shut up."

Max's stumbling explanation for his quick capitulation told Wyatt his guess was right. This was the man in charge, the real brains behind the operation he knew Max hadn't been smart enough to mastermind. He'd probably been ordered to cozy up to Jordan, to get the boy to quiz him on the setup at HP.

"We'll go get the stuff now, finish the job—"

"I said, shut up." The man's voice was cold, and as vaguely familiar as his face. "You've served your purpose."

"I caught the boy," Max said, sounding desperate now, "I heard him up here in the trees, Mr. Stark, and—"

The man shot him in the face.

Jordan yelped in terror as Max collapsed soundlessly in front of him. The boy backed up hastily but stumbled, and Stark was on him before he could recover. The casualness of the murder, and the speed with which he did it and then shifted his aim back to Jordan, was chilling. He clamped a hand on the boy's shoulder and yanked him to his feet.

But just as chilling was the name Max had used, the name that had pulled together that vague familiarity of face and voice.

Phillip Stark.

Odd that he'd thought about him not that long ago, the crime boss whose son, also a killer with a minimal claim on sanity, had died during an operation three years ago. His father, this man, had gone to prison himself. Not for long enough; although he'd been the mastermind again, they hadn't been able to prove it, and he'd been convicted on much lesser charges. And there'd been sympathy, however undeserved, for the man who'd just lost his son. The man who so publicly and emotionally wailed over the death of a son who had, in his short but productive career, murdered at least nine people in cold blood, probably more.

Like father, like son....

He'd gotten five years. And been released after three. And that ludicrous inequity, in a system that was supposed to bring justice, had been the beginning of the end for Wyatt.

"At last, Agent Blake," Stark said with deep satisfaction.

He should never have put all those odd inquiries on the back burner, Wyatt thought. Because suddenly it all made sense, the flurry of inquiries from people, people who could come across as friendlies, people he'd helped over the years. No doubt approached by this man, posing perhaps as another of them with a good, benevolent reason to want to find and thank the agent that had helped him in some way. Or maybe, since his face wasn't unknown, he'd had someone else do it. Some other dupe like Max, who was probably also dead by now. But either way, Wyatt guessed he'd been looking for him ever since he'd gotten out.

It was all Wyatt could do not to launch himself at the man. But he had no doubt the man wouldn't hesitate to shoot, he'd just proven that, and right now his weapon was jammed against Jordan's ear.

If he could distract him, give Jordan a chance to run, get to Kai, she'd help him, Wyatt knew that down to his bones. But there was no guarantee he could take the shot that would inevitably come and keep moving long enough to give Jordan a chance to get away. Besides, he knew too damned well he was rusty. Rusty enough to cost his son his life? Had he slowed down that much, been away from the game too long?

Possible, he thought grimly. Too possible.

All this tumbled through Wyatt's mind in rapid succession. But above it all stood one imperative that outweighed all the rest.

Jordan.

He had to get Jordan away from the man. He raced through every bit of information he could remember about the man, searching for a tool he could use. He grabbed the first one that occurred to him, because he didn't have time to think of others.

He looked at the man with what he hoped was a puzzled expression. And prayed he'd picked the right button to push.

"Do I know you?"

The reaction would have been almost comical had the man not had a gun on Jordan, who was struggling manfully not to show how scared he had to be.

Stark swore, sharply. "You bastard, you ruin my life, you kill my son and you don't even remember me?"

Right button, Wyatt thought. And interesting what order he put things in. You'd think the loss of a son would come first.

It hit him then, hard and fast, exactly what this was all about. It was a leap, but he knew in his gut, that gut that had never failed him back when dealing with this sort of human debris had been his job, that he was right.

This had never been about drugs at all, or stealing those materials.

From the start, this had been about getting to him.

Payback.

A son for a son.

He was going to kill Jordan. And he was going to make Wyatt watch him do it.

Chapter 27

Hidden back in the trees, Kai barely breathed, terrified the stranger with the gun might hear. Although the hammering of her heart seemed so loud to her she was amazed all three of the people in that horrible, moonlit tableau didn't turn to look.

She'd seriously regretted her decision to walk tonight. She'd known the moment Jordy took off on his bike that she was going to have a hard time keeping up with him. Still, it was easier in the woods than if he'd been on the road. But it was also scarier; in the moonlight everything looked spooky. She clung to the distant red dot of his bike's taillight like a beacon.

She had realized, once she oriented herself, where Jordy was headed. HP was the only thing out here, in this literal neck of the woods. It all came together for her then; Wyatt gone unexpectedly, leaving Jordy behind, apparently locked in, and now the boy breaking out and heading for HP.

Max.

Wyatt must have seen something earlier, something that Max had done, that told him tonight was the night.

He had been right, all along. Those suspicions that had so angered her in the beginning had been right on, just misdirected at first. He might have left the work, but he still had the instincts of a pro.

Jordy looked so scared. The stranger, with his back to her, had the boy held tight against his left side, so that while she couldn't see the stranger's face, she could see Jordy's. And the gun rammed against his right ear.

But he also looked stunned, no doubt at the incredible transformation of the most boring guy in the world. He was staring at his father in utter shock. She couldn't blame him. Even she, who had been somewhat prepared, barely recognized the man she saw. She'd seen glimpses, especially in the suspicious man who had first come into her store, but nothing like this. And any doubt she'd had that everything David had found out was the truth vanished.

If I was a bad guy, I'd give up just to stop him looking at me like that, she thought.

She wondered how many of those bad guys he'd put away with just that look.

A federal cop. It was still stunning to her, too. As did her certainty, even without any explanation, that if Wyatt truly had killed this man's son, it was with good reason.

"Before, I was just going to track you down and kill you," the man said to Wyatt. "Now, watching you watch me slaughter your own son will be so much more delicious."

Kai shivered involuntarily at the very idea that anyone could use those words about the murder of a child. Jordy whimpered, and her chest tightened at the sound. Yet Wyatt's face betrayed little; had she not come to know him so well she'd never have seen the emotion in the set of his jaw and the intensity of his gaze, fastened on the man who held his son.

"You so much as scratch him, and you're a dead man."

Wyatt's voice was cold, so cold that she couldn't see why the man didn't start shivering just like she was.

Maybe because he's so cold inside already, she thought. You'd have to be, to use a child, to threaten a child like that. She should do something, find a rock, a big stick, *something,* but she had no idea what she could do against a gun.

The other man snorted. "Always the hero, aren't you, Blake? I met a few other people in prison who had you to blame for destroying their lives."

"Your beef is with me," Wyatt said. "I'll make you a deal."

"You have nothing to bargain with, Blake. I hold all the cards." He tightened his grip on Jordy's shoulder so much the boy went white. But he made no sound. In fact, Kai thought, the set of his jaw made him suddenly look more like his father than ever.

"I'm the one who killed your son. You let the boy go, and take me. I'll go without a fight."

"Self-sacrifice? How noble of you." He shook Jordy. "Isn't that touching? Your father's willing to die in your place."

Jordy made an unintelligible sound. But he was staring at his father a whole new way yet again.

"If you knew enough to find us, you know we barely know each other," Wyatt said. "He hates me. Kill me and he'll think you did him a favor, and never say a word."

Wyatt said it matter-of-factly, like a man who believed it completely. Her heart nearly broke for him. He'd been trying so hard. She thought there'd been a small bit of progress, a slight softening in Jordy's attitude, but obviously Wyatt didn't believe it.

"Well, well. Perhaps he's smarter than I thought. But nevertheless, an eye for an eye. Shall I start there, with his eyes? They are rather like yours."

Kai gasped, unable to quite smother it. Again she was amazed they all didn't turn to look.

Turn to look.

As she thought the words, David's voice suddenly echoed in her mind.

Heavy training, tactics, weapons...

Then her own thought. *The instincts of a pro.*

She took a deep breath. Perhaps it wasn't the wisest thing, but it was the only thing she could think of that she could do. She just had to trust it would be enough.

Wyatt kept his gaze fastened on Stark's face. On his eyes, eyes that would betray intent in the instant before he was going to shoot.

And Wyatt had no doubt the man would shoot. Because insanity also lurked in those eyes, just as it had in the man's son, who had taken great pleasure in not just kidnapping and killing but torturing and carving up his victims with a blade that made Max's look like a butter knife.

Jordan squirmed against the tight grip. Wyatt's breath caught in his throat.

"Don't move, Jordy," he said.

The boy froze. For an instant their gazes locked, although his aim at Stark never wavered. Those eyes, so like his own, looked back at him with a steadiness that made his heart pound. Was there more of him in his son than he'd ever realized? Had he been so loaded down with the weight of it, with the concept of having a child he was suddenly responsible for, that he'd never really looked at that child as an individual?

And if this goes south, you'll never get the chance, he thought grimly.

He'd just better make damned sure if it did go south, he—and Stark—were the only casualties.

Wyatt knew all the numbers, what fraction of time that Stark would still be able to pull the trigger depending on where in the head he shot him. He knew what his best target was, knew what the chances were.

He didn't like any of it. Not when Jordan was the one most at risk.

A sound came out of the shadows. From back in the trees. A voice. Not talking, or even yelling, but…singing. A glorious, beautiful burst of sound.

Kai.

He thought the name, felt the recognition well

up in him like a joyous greeting, in the split second before Stark reacted. The man jerked around, shocked surprise on his face.

His grip on Jordan loosened.

The barrel of his pistol slipped to the side.

Just enough.

Wyatt fired.

Stark went down. Jordan screamed. Jumped away. Stark lay motionless. Wyatt recognized the limpness inherent only to the dead. He wasn't quite as rusty as he'd feared.

It was over.

Chapter 28

"That was insane. He could have killed you."

Kai looked at Wyatt. She had herself back under control now, the wild shaking that had overtaken her in those first moments after her hastily conceived ploy had worked receding.

She heard the anger that made his voice razor sharp. But she knew him now, well enough to know what that anger was triggered by. And he was shaken enough himself that he let it show in his face; pure relief. It was that Jordy was safe, she knew, but she didn't think it was egotistic to assume some of that relief was for her, too.

He stood with his arm around Jordy, who was allowing it without comment. The boy was pale, even in the moonlight, clearly stunned and apparently unaware that his father had carefully urged him around so his back was to the bodies. Another shiver went through her; she'd never been even remotely close to anything like this, and it would rattle her into paralysis if she let it. She couldn't let it. Not yet.

"I'm insane?" she said, letting incredulity into her tone. "You're the one who took this on alone. What would have happened to Jordy if you'd gotten yourself killed? Did you even think of that?"

His brow furrowed, as if he were merely puzzled. "Of course I did. That's why I brought a second gun."

And that, she supposed, said it all. And in effect, made her point. "Exactly. That's why I figured," she said with a level look at Wyatt, "that all a highly trained federal agent would need would be a slight distraction."

Wyatt's eyes widened a fraction. He drew back slightly, wariness leaping back to life almost palpably as she saw him process that she knew who—and what—he was. Jordy yelped in shock; what he'd seen had to have de-

stroyed his perception of his father, but obviously he hadn't quite put all the pieces together
yet in his stunned young mind.

"Kai," Wyatt began, sounding beyond uncomfortable.

"Yes," she said. "You have a lot of explaining
to do. To both of us."

"I never meant to lie to you," he said, his
voice barely a whisper. "I just… I'm not that
man anymore."

"You're wrong, Wyatt," she said softly.
"If I've learned nothing else about you, I've
learned that. Once a hero, always a hero. Even
if you don't want to be."

"I'm no—"

"Don't even try to deny that one," she said.
"You proved it tonight, even if there weren't
sixteen years of other heroics before now."

She had shifted her gaze to Jordy as she
spoke, saw his eyes widen even further. She
was guessing the boy had learned many, many
lessons tonight, and that it was going to take a
good, long time for him to sort it all out. But
right now it was enough that he turned to look
up at his father with awe and a raging curiosity.

Which left her to figure out how she felt about landing in a spot she never expected to be in. In love with a cop of sorts. And one who would ever and always end up being that hero.

Even when, like some Old West gunfighter who'd hung up his guns, he tried not to be.

Dealing with all the mess, statements to the authorities and late-arriving cavalry, explanations to his boss, was time-consuming, exhausting and undeniably familiar. And he'd do it all ten times over to avoid what was to come.

What he'd seen in Jordan's eyes and in Kai's face had sparked more emotion than he'd had to deal with in a very long time. His son, and the nervy, gutsy woman who'd risked herself to help them, had turned his quest for peace and boredom upside down.

And he knew Kai had been right.

He had some explaining to do, to both of the people he loved.

He nearly shuddered inwardly at the simple fact that he had used the word, and that he'd meant it. The realization shocked him almost as much as his own actions had shocked his son.

There was so much to work out, so much to talk about. With a capital *T,* as Kai had put it.

The thought made him smile. And suddenly the burden seemed lighter. And for the first time in a very long time, he felt the desire to do just that, work it all out.

Wyatt wasn't sure exactly what John had said to the investigators, but he was a more than solid citizen whose standing in the community expedited the process. He knew there would be more to come but for now, there was a lull.

And sooner than he'd expected—and sooner than he'd have liked, he admitted, calling himself a coward in the process—he was back to facing the music.

The old phrase ran through his mind before he thought, and then it made him smile. Music indeed. Kai's music may have moved hundreds of thousands, even millions, but he'd bet he and Jordan were the only ones who could say it had literally saved their lives.

He walked out of the HP office where the interviews had been taking place, and back to John's private anteroom. He opened the door, and for a moment just stood there, looking at the woman and the boy who were waiting. His son stood up, his eyes wide and full of tangled emotions Wyatt could only imagine were reflected in his own.

"Jordy," he said, his voice tight. Then, catching himself, he corrected it. "Sorry. Jordan."

"It's all right," the boy said, his voice quiet. He flicked a glance at Kai. "She…told me. What you used to be. The stuff you did, people you saved."

Wyatt's breath died in his throat. She really did know. He shifted his glance to Kai.

"You can be angry if you want, that I told him," she said. "But it was purely selfish."

"Selfish?"

"I wanted your explaining to be why, not what."

He closed his eyes. Drew in a long breath. Lowered his head. He couldn't do this.

He had no choice. No more than he had last night.

He had to do this. She had the right. And she hadn't said it, never would in front of Jordy, but she'd had the right to know before she'd gone to bed with him. Any woman had the right to know who she was really sleeping with. Not that they'd ever done much sleeping in those fiery afternoon hours.

He had to do this.

"My life then," he said, his voice low and harsh, "was full of people like Stark. And the ones they harmed were never the same, after. For a long time it was enough, to put the bad ones away. But…it never ended. No matter how bad one guy was, there was always another who was worse."

He opened his eyes then, saw them both looking at him. Quietly listening, as if his words were going to determine the course of all their lives.

Maybe they were.

He started again. "When they only sentenced Stark to five years, I knew I was done. When they let him out of jail early, I knew it was the right decision."

"You knew he was out?" Kai asked.

He nodded.

"Had he…threatened you? Before?"

The memory of the day Stark had been dragged out of court screaming about what he would do to Wyatt when he got out was particularly clear in his mind at the moment.

"Yes." Kai gave him a look that wasn't too hard to interpret. "Why wasn't I more on guard?"

"If you knew," she began.

He sighed. "He was just the latest in a long line vowing payback. I tracked them, but if I assumed every one would follow through, I'd be living in a cave somewhere, with a machine gun."

"How did he find you?"

"He did come up with a unique approach."

"Unique?"

"He used friendlies."

She blinked. "What?"

"He approached some people, civilians, who…had reason to be friendly. Pretended to be one of them."

"People you'd helped."

"Yes."

Kai flicked a glance at Jordy, who was watching and listening silently. But at least it was an avid sort of silence, not the sullen withdrawal he'd been used to.

"People," she said, "whose lives you'd saved. Or whose loved ones you'd saved."

His mouth quirked. Was she trying to build him up in front of his son? "Some," he admitted. "People known to the team, people they'd be more inclined to be open with."

"They told them where you were?"

He shook his head. "They wouldn't. But apparently he got little bits from enough people, through the friendlies he cultivated, getting them to call and ask about me, under the guise of being…thankful. Eventually, he got enough."

"You knew this."

"I hadn't put it all together yet, but yes."

"Why didn't you ask for help?"

"I cut all my ties with that world. I even cashed out my retirement, so there'd be no trail to me."

"I mean from me," she said, startling him. "I thought we were…close enough."

Fire shot through him at the images sparked by her careful words. She didn't look at Jordy, but he knew they were both painfully aware of the boy's presence.

She had every right, he supposed. They were sleeping together, they'd shared the most intimate moments he'd ever known, but he'd never told her the truth.

"I'm…used to doing things on my own. I've never had much choice. Until now."

"And?"

"Now I don't want to do it that way anymore. But I have to learn how…not to." He glanced at Jordy. "And how not to be like my father."

It was confused, convoluted, and as usual, Kai understood perfectly. The smile she gave him told him that. And then and there he made a silent promise to her—and his son—that he would learn, somehow.

Kai would help him. He knew that now, knew it bone deep.

"Why didn't you ever tell me?" It was the first thing Jordy had said since this started. "Why did you let me keep thinking you were this boring old guy?"

"Because that's what I wanted to be."

Jordy frowned. "But why?" Then the frown vanished as something occurred to him. "You never told because you didn't want him to find you?"

"Us."

Jordy blinked. "Oh." Then, in a voice with a slight tinge of hurt this time, "Why didn't my mom ever tell me?"

Ouch. He'd figured that one was coming, and felt as if he'd opened the door on a roomful of time bombs, all set to go off simultaneously. How the hell did he explain a promise of no-strings sex to a thirteen-year-old?

"I never asked her not to," he said. "I'm sure she had her reasons." He took a breath, glanced at Kai, who gave him a barely perceptible nod. Trusting her, he plunged ahead. "Just like she had her reasons for never telling me about you."

"Until she was dying," Jordy said. It was a measure of his state of mind, Wyatt guessed, that for the first time he said it baldly, out loud, without a quiver in his voice.

"Yes."

"Then she had no choice. You didn't want to be my father."

"Didn't plan on it," Wyatt admitted. "There's a difference."

"And he went from that," Kai said softly, but still drawing Jordy's attention, "to being willing to die for you last night."

Jordy's eyes widened, as if he'd forgotten that part. His gaze shot back to his father's face. "You really would have traded with me?"

His first instinct was to dissemble, brush it off, pretend the situation hadn't been as dire as it had been. But something in the way Kai had said it made him change his mind.

"In an instant," he said, as softly as she had.

The look of wonder that came into the eyes that were like looking in a younger mirror told him he'd made the right call.

While you're on a roll, he thought, and looked at Kai.

"Just like I'd do for Kai," he said, just as softly. "In an instant."

He'd caught her off guard, hard enough to do that it pleased him when she first gaped, then, very slowly, smiled that smile that set off urgent fires all through him.

"You're sure about that?" she asked.

He nodded. "It's what a man does, when he… loves somebody." Her breath caught audibly. He reached out and brushed his fingers over her cheek. "But if you *ever* take a chance like you did last night again…"

She reached up and cupped his hand, holding it to her face. "It's what a woman does, when she loves somebody. Takes a chance."

Wyatt felt an odd sort of tumble inside at her words. He hadn't realized how much he'd let himself hope until she said them.

"I'm a hell of a long shot, Kai. I don't know how to…be with someone."

"You didn't know how to be a father, either, but you're coming right along. Trainable is good."

One corner of his mouth quirked. He wanted to grab her, kiss her senseless, but he had one more thing he had to get out. He was aware that Jordy was standing there, staring at them, he could almost feel the boy's mind racing, processing, as if he were trying to figure out if what he was hearing meant what it sounded like.

"Besides," Kai said softly, "we have a lot

in common. We both gave up something we loved, because we couldn't take what came with it anymore."

He'd never thought of it that way before. Leave it to Kai to put it in a way that made so much sense.

"There could be more where Stark came from," he said, finally getting out that last warning.

"At least now I'll be prepared. But one thing, Wyatt."

"Only one?"

"For now."

"What?"

She glanced at Jordy then. "No more hiding. Anything from anyone."

"Agreed," he said instantly, meaning it.

They turned to face the boy who had, in his way, brought them together. He was staring at them both.

"You all right with this?" Wyatt asked.

Jordy looked from him to Kai and back again. "You?" he asked, very tentatively.

"Us," Kai confirmed.

"You mean like…together? The two of you?"

"I was hoping," Kai said, "it would be more like the three of us."

Jordy's jaw dropped. He swallowed visibly. He looked at his father. "You mean it?"

"More than I've ever meant anything," Wyatt said. "Turns out I'm not quite through with life, after all."

Jordy stared at them, speechless. Kai took pity on him. "You've had way too much thrown at you in way too short a time, haven't you? Why don't you go round us up some sodas from that machine out in the hall?"

The practicality of that seemed to distract the boy. "I don't have any money."

Wyatt reached into his pocket and pulled out what he had and handed most of it over. Still, Jordy hesitated.

"I'm about to kiss her, if that makes up your mind," he said.

"Ew," Jordy said, and wheeled around to dart through the door.

Wyatt laughed, for the first time in what seemed like forever. He pulled her against him. "Why did you pick that song?"

She blinked. As if it took her a moment to even remember.

"It was the only thing that would come out. It's been in my mind, I guess," she said.

As it had been in his. "Playing With Fire."

"I'm not playing," he said. "Not anymore."

"Does that mean you're to make good on that promise to kiss me?" Kai asked, rather archly.

He turned back to her, feeling an almost unbearable tightness in his chest as he looked at the woman who had burned through his walls so effortlessly.

"I'm going to make good on all of them," he said. "But I'll start with that one."

And he did.

* * * * *

Mills & Boon® Online

Discover more romance at
www.millsandboon.co.uk

 FREE online reads

 Books up to one
month before shops

 Browse our books
before you buy

...and much more!

For exclusive competitions and instant updates:

Like us on **facebook.com/romancehq**

Follow us on **twitter.com/millsandboonuk**

Join us on **community.millsandboon.co.uk**

*Visit us
Online*
Sign up for our FREE eNewsletter at
www.millsandboon.co.uk

WEB/M&B/RTL4/LP